The Sabbath

Arthur Nsenga
&
Shaunakay Francis

IN LOVING MEMORY
OF
BIENAIMÉ SHEMBO
1991-2013

Acknowledgments

To God be the glory
Amen.

1

"I'm calling in sick tomorrow," Lana whispered as she shivered into Cory's car and fumbled with the heating. "There's no way I will make it to work in the morning. I'm drunk, and it's already four a.m."

Cory started the car and lowered the music. "Yeah, you should have just given your shift away," he teased.

Lana gave him a look, too tired and full of Denny's late-night pancakes to respond. If not for him, she would have been spending this cool Saturday morning in June snuggled up in her bed; instead, she had her arms folded, staring at the side-view mirror, wondering how she'd let Cory persuade her to go to a house party on a work night.

Truth is, it took little convincing; Lana had been nursing a small crush on Cory for quite a while now. The only problem was she valued their friendship more than the prospect of romance, so she never acted on her feelings. Plus, Cory hid his emotions so well Lana did not know if her feelings would be returned. Rather than pondering their relationship for the hundredth time, she turned up the radio, losing herself in the music as Cory sped down the calm and quiet main street.

"I'm sleeping over; I'm way too tired to drive home," Cory announced as he pulled into Lana's apartment driveway.

"Yeah, sure," she replied, half-asleep, although she wanted her bed to herself. She yearned to crawl half-naked into crisp clean sheets and sleep until three in the afternoon.

Lana got out of the car, dropping her purse as she did so.

"Ugghhh," she muttered, stumbling like a dipsomaniac to pick it up, her little black dress and six-inch heels added to the difficulty.

She stood up and sighed, then glanced up at the sky, wondering if the sun was rising already. It was a little too bright outside, considering it was before dawn. She froze, unable to speak or even move.

The sky was on fire.

Amazed and confused, Lana stood there, trying to remember if any meteorite showers were scheduled to happen today, when her thoughts were interrupted by the flash of a large flaming object sailing through the air, followed by another, and another.

Soon the sky surged with huge fiery rocks crashing through the atmosphere. There were thousands of them. The entire sky was a blazing inferno. Lana sensed danger, but she was in a trance - too terrified and astonished to do anything but stare in wonder at the beauty of the dancing shades of red, orange, and blue.

There was a thunderous bang as fireballs erupted like Fourth of July fireworks, becoming more horrifying than entrancing. Another rock exploded, disintegrating into millions of pieces - some mere dust, while the rest came crashing down like fiery hailstones. A few splinters, no bigger than a handful of broken eggshells, struck Lana on her forehead almost knocking her down, but the alcohol in her system rendered her numb to the pain. She sensed a quick burst of warmth as they bounced off her and onto the ground.

A howling wind picked up, throwing burning hailstones down harder and faster.

BOOM!

Another enormous bang, followed by yet another burst of blazing stones, filled the heavens. Lana panicked as one by one, the fireballs transformed into deadly projectiles, piercing the night sky.

"Lana...Lana...Lana"

Even through the roar of the smoking skies, she could hear Cory and turned to see him running toward her, nostrils flaring and eyes bulging. Lana had never seen fear from Cory, but still, it did nothing to tear her from the theatrical display in the night sky. She looked back up to the bleeding sky, glued to the spectacle.

"We need to - to go - inside!" he stuttered, his voice loud and trembling. "These rocks will kill us!"

Unable to find her voice, Lana let Cory drag her by the arm into her apartment, not sure whether what she had just witnessed had been real or not.

2

Something was wrong. Lana's body felt too heavy. It was an immense struggle just to open her eyes. She sat up in bed, surveying her surroundings. Lana's table was still stacked high with expensive chemical engineering textbooks; her papers and current assignments teetered over her laptop, which was peeking out from underneath the mess.

Her closet was neat and organized; clothes and shoes lined up in order of color. Everything appeared to be just how she left it, but she couldn't shake the visceral feeling something wasn't right. To make matters worse, Lana couldn't remember what she had been doing before she went to bed.

She took a calming breath as she noticed Cory stretched out asleep beside her. At least now, she knew she had been well looked after, but Lana didn't remember him sleeping over either. Again, she tried to recall what she had done the night before. She wanted to wake him for answers, but she checked her phone instead. The time on her phone read 4:45 am.

That's odd, she thought. She had never awoken at five o'clock in the morning before, but she felt rested and full of energy, as if she'd slept for days. Lana chuckled; her grandmother always complained about her not getting enough sleep. *I wonder if Grandma is up jogging yet,* Lana questioned while scrolling through her phone calls.

Lana's grandmother had raised her since the tender age of nine. That's when her mother decided pursuing a successful career took precedence over a relationship with her daughter. Lana's father was a chief commander in the army, but knew nothing about being a father. He would not spend more than a few days at a time with Lana, and as she grew older, he stopped coming home altogether.

Her grandmother had been both her mother and father for as long as she could remember. Despite their age difference, she and Lana were best of friends. When Lana moved for college, they'd vowed to each other to speak every day, even if just to say good morning or goodnight.

Her grandmother lived in British Columbia, which was several days' car travel away from Lana. Her grandmother looked too young to have a twenty-year-old granddaughter, or at least, that was what she told everyone. Truth is, at sixty-two years of age, she was an active and vibrant woman. She looked more like forty-five, and every chance she got, she reminded everyone she had middle-aged women beat. She knew how to keep her looks, but that's not enough to keep a man.

Giovanni was her fourth and her current husband. He was a rich Italian, who owned a chain of offshore oil fields. Lana hated the man for the way he threw his money around, but for the sake of her grandmother, she played nice and went along with his irritating ways. He made an effort, but Lana swore he tried to hard to connect to her grandmother's nationality. Taking them on trips to Jamaica did not win Lana over - even though she loved going there and wished she could just stay there all winter long.

Lana's heartbeat accelerated as she noticed the date on her phone. She was missing a whole day of data. *On the twenty-fifth, I spoke to Grandma at 9:06am before I went to class. I didn't get to say goodnight to her because I closed at work and then went to the party with Cory.*

She gasped. *Oh yes, the party with Cory. I should have spoken to her on the twenty-sixth. I should have spoken to Jay, Lisa, or any number of people. But there's nothing here. It's as if I didn't use my phone all day.*

She had to work on the twenty-sixth. *Did I even call off of work?*

Lana checked her call log and realized she hadn't.

There's no way I could have slept for twenty-four hours...

Running her fingers through her hair, she winced as her hand brushed her forehead. Shaking her head, she took a deep calming breath, then fumbled with the screen as she checked her social media sites. Other people should have posted something yesterday.

The world can't just not do anything for a day! It's hard enough to get people to take part in Earth Hour. They can't survive without being socialites for a day.

Her mind raced as she strove to convince herself that everything was normal. However, she found the same thing happening on her social networks. It was now the 27th, and none of her friends or followers had any posts from the 26th until now.

It must be my connection. Pinning her hope on that logic, she dialed Cory's number.

Within seconds, his phone rang near the bedside. After the first ring, she hung up. Jumping to grab her laptop from the table, the paper stacks went sprawling onto the floor. Her computer's date read the 27th and so did every website she visited.

So she had slept through a full day.

She called her grandmother; she needed to hear her as well as get confirmation. Her call went straight to voicemail. Something was wrong.

Cory needs to wake up now.

She called his name, but he seemed just as fast asleep as he had been a moment ago, so she shook him instead.

"Cory, wake up. Something weird is going on." She tried shaking him again. "Cory. I think the entire world fell asleep for a whole day. Wake up. Cor…" She stopped. A cold chill crept up her spine and rested on the nape of her neck. She froze. Memories flooded back, and she recalled those final events, right before she had lost consciousness. Lana stumbled to the window; she pulled the curtains away, her jaw dropping at the sight.

"Cory. I swear if you don't wake up…" she yelled, turning back to Cory as he stirred in bed.

Lana surveyed her lawn again. Even in the dim light of dawn, she saw it was covered with chunks of shiny, dark, metallic-looking rocks, piling deeper where they had cascaded off the roof. She knew where they came from—the combustible meteorites that had shot out of the sky.

But that was twenty-four hours ago - what had happened during that time? And did everybody else lose a day? Not just those who kept a social media presence, too?

Lana, now annoyed with Cory, climbed onto her bed and from a standing position, gave Cory a hard kick that knocked him onto the hardwood floor with a loud thud.

"Ow! Fuck!" His 6-foot-4 physique sprawled across the floor. His brown eyes and mocha skin looked refreshed, a lot more defined than usual.

I wonder if my skin looks that good right now… maybe sleep does make you look better and healthier… She caught a glimpse of herself in the dresser mirror, but then her mind trailed off as she sat down on the bed and stared at

Cory.

He turned to glare up at her in utter disbelief.

"Are you serious right now? Was that called for?" he boomed, still half-asleep.

"You need to wake up. Something is seriously going on. We've lost the last twenty-four hours of our life, and there are black rocks scattered everywhere - not to mention the shower of meteorites that started the whole thing." She was becoming hysterical. "Don't look at me like that. Get up, right now."

Cory blinked a few times, trying to gather his thoughts. He sprang up from the floor in one fluid motion, and took several steps toward the window, then walked back to Lana.

He traced his finger around the lump on her forehead, his eyes gazing into hers, opened his mouth to speak, but to no avail. Lana just shrugged her shoulders, and Cory, in his speechless state, froze, his expression wearing concern as if it had been etched into his core.

As everything began to sink in, Cory became consumed by the many thoughts running through his mind. Finally, he spoke.

"Either the world is about to end, or the Government is about to fuck up our lives. Either way, I need to get home to my mom; she's probably terrified and prophesying that we're going to start hearing trumpets and the coming of Christ."

Lana rolled her eyes. Cory could be so dramatic, and always made his mother seem more spiritual than she was - but Lana thought she was pretty cool. She wasn't like those crazy religious women who found God and thought they didn't need a man. And right now, if Cory's mother was preaching about the coming of Christ, she might be right.

Something *was* coming. Lana sensed this. It might not be Christ, but whatever it was, it was most definitely not anything good. There was no mistaking the persistent chill she felt creeping up her spine.

Still doubtful about what she had said, Cory looked at his own phone to check the date, and his heart dropped. Lana was right. An entire day had gone by, and they hadn't even noticed. He checked to see if his mother attempted to contact him since the day of the party. Not a text or call – nothing. He dialed home in a hurry, expecting to hear the voice of his sister, Isabel, who should be there taking care of their mother.

No answer.

He tried his sister's cell phone, but his calls went straight to voicemail. Cory was apprehensive, and rightfully so. His mother had been going through chemotherapy to treat breast cancer this past month. The treatment made her very weak and for the last few days, she had been confined to her bed. Had it not been for Isabel, Cory would be at his mother's side, making sure she was okay. But it was wrong to blame Isabel for his absence. She had convinced Cory to go out because she feared that Cory's depression was progressing at a much faster rate than their mother's illness.

Cory feared what this strange extended sleep could do to his mother's body. *What if she didn't have the strength to wake up after twenty-four hours? She could be in a coma or worse,* he thought.

"I've got to go home," he told Lana.

"I'm not staying here by myself. I'm coming with you."

3

An awkward silence hung between the two as they climbed into Cory's car. The wall of tension had become so high that neither of them were willing to overcome it to comfort the other one. Cory did his best to keep his composure, but he felt his life hanging from a thread, ready to snap free at the slightest disturbance. He didn't know what he would do if anything bad happened to his mother, and that thought alone tore him apart inside. Sensing his frustration, Lana gave in and placed her hand on Cory's shoulder, offering him her support.

"Cory, everything will be all right. I bet they're still sleeping," she said.

Cory ignored her and kept driving. His windshield had a jagged crack starting to run along its base, and bits of black dust and small pebbles clattered hard against it as they drove off. He made a sharp right turn then stomped on the brake. At least twenty cars rammed into each other; and dozens of people injured in major collisions now blocking the intersection. Smashed windshields became deadly glass projectiles, and many passengers were laying unconscious on car hoods, thrown about like rag dolls. Others stood in confusion, trying to make sense of their situation. The wind carried the sound of agony of broken bones, burnt skin, and mothers crying out for help while holding onto their motionless children.

Shards of glass covered the road like Christmas snow. A burning smell lingered in the air, meeting any oncoming traffic. Lana rolled down her window and waved at a knot of people on the sidewalk.

"Hey, what happened here?" she hollered.

A young lady, no older than eighteen, made her way to their car. She was slender, her pale face streaked with dried blood from her cuts, framed by blonde hair tied back into a scraggly bun. Her unblinking brown eyes were open wide, and she shivered as the strong breeze blew right through her dirty blue sweater.

"Nobody knows what happened," she said, her voice choking. "I was sleeping on the bus when all of a sudden I woke up to everybody screaming. I didn't realize how serious it was until I saw my own blood. That's when I panicked… I got out of there so fast, but it's even more chaotic out here."

Her body trembled as she took a calming deep breath.

"You all right?" Cory asked.

"Yes…but everyone here is paranoid, things don't make sense…"

"All right, okay," Cory interrupted.

Cory knew where the conversation was heading, and he didn't need the added stress. Without a second to waste, he turned the car around and took a different route home. As they got closer to his house, it became evident that something was dreadfully wrong. Car accidents jammed the roads at major intersection, and people staggered about, their cries echoing through the streets.

"What the fuck is going on," Cory cried out.

Lana stared at him in disbelief, while gnawing her fingernail. She had lost the certainty everything would "be all right," and her thoughts raced a mile a minute. She didn't know what to say.

It was still early in the morning when they reached Cory's house. Lana couldn't shake the sense of something not being right, and was hoping his mother and sister were inside sleeping.

"Mom…Isabel?" Cory yelled as he entered his home.

No response came.

"Go check my sister's room," he ordered Lana, as he took the stairs two at a time up to his mother's room on the second floor. Stopping at the door, he knocked, his voice quiet and cautious, "Mom, are you there?"

There was still no answer.

He wanted to rip open the door to check on his sick mother, but he feared what he might find. He took a moment to prepare himself for the worst.

Why aren't they answering? What if mom is in a coma after sleeping for that long…can that even happen?

Footsteps creeping up the stairs interrupted his thoughts. He turned to find Isabel and Lana coming toward him. Despite everything, Isabel looked well rested in her large purple robe, with her hair tied up in a silk head wrap. He let out a sigh of relief and in that moment, relaxed a little. Seeing his sister awake gave him the confirmation he needed to believe everything was all right.

"Cory, it's too early in the morning. What's going on?" Isabel whispered.

Trying to preserve his newfound optimism, he decided not to mention the night of the fiery skies, and the twenty-four hours gone from their lives.

"I'm just worried about mother, that's all," he replied.

"Well, she's sleeping...try not to wake her, will ya?"

"I won't - was just going to make sure she's comfortable."

Cory grabbed the knob and eased the door open, trying not to startle his mother. Taking one step into the room, he froze. His head pounded like a jackhammer as his heartbeat went haywire. He took in ragged gulps of air. The time came to a complete halt, there in the doorway, and his worst fears boiled up and tormented him.

She was not there.

"What's wrong?"

He heard voices in the background, but his brain refused to process them. Giving no answer, he spun around and bolted from the room. He was now a man on a mission, methodically checking every room in the house. Finally, back in his mother's room, he collapsed on the floor, his head and arms resting on her bed.

No longer in control of his emotions, tears poured from his eyes, streaming down his cheeks and onto the flowery bedspread. Digging his face deeper into his mother's bed, he noticed the bed was cold. He lifted his head to find Lana standing in the corner comforting his sobbing sister.

Glancing at Cory, Lana saw the expression of rage on his face. Balling up his fists, he approached them, bellowing,

"Where the fuck is she, Isabel?"

Lana jumped to block his path.

"Cory, stop," Lana ordered, stretching out her arms. "This isn't her fault."

She tried calming him, but it was like talking to a brick wall. She feared for Isabel as his emotions got the better of him. With one sweep of his hand, Cory brushed Lana aside and seized his sister.

"Where is she?" he screamed, shaking Isabel like a pit-bull shakes its prey. The terrified girl was speechless, and Cory knew he was hurting her. He wanted to stop, but his out of control feelings wouldn't let him. He was only concerned with finding his mother.

Suddenly, his mother's voice echoed in the back of his head. *Cory, your temper will be the death of you!* - Something she always said to him when he lost his cool. He took a step back from Isabel, and the anxiety left him.

Isabel looked more scared and confused than her brother. Her eyes were bloodshot from crying. Her body was shaking, and her lips trembled, making it difficult for her to speak.

"I-I-I put her to bed. I swear!" she said, with a stutter.

Cory grabbed her again, but this time he held her tight, overwhelmed by the guilt he felt for blaming Isabel for their mother's disappearance. Everything had hit him all at once. He needed to process his thoughts and figure out what happened and, most specifically, what happened to his invalid mother.

Sitting Isabel down, he told her everything that had happened to them in the past forty-eight hours. It wasn't long before she broke down in tears again.

"I don't understand," Isabel mumbled through a continuous stream of sobs. "She went to bed at eleven. She should be here."

As soon as Isabel was calm enough, they went downstairs.

"Let's see if the TV is working," Lana suggested. "Someone must be reporting this."

Every channel was covering the fiery light show in the sky, followed by the mystifying twenty-four hours time gap. It had happened all over the world, and they were calling the phenomenon, "The Sabbath." Although the news didn't provide them with any real answers, it comforted them knowing they weren't the only ones going through this mayhem.

The news pleaded for people not to overload the switchboards and police stations with missing persons reports, and instead urged everyone to stay home and wait there. They suggested waiting for at least twenty-four hours before contacting authorities, and to expect long delays. Emergency personnel would be stretched thin attending to and finding the wounded, and responding to the growing reports of fatalities.

Cory and Isabel had no choice but to wait out the time. They sat in the living room, glued to the TV, hoping to receive more information on what was happening to their world.

4

Initial reports from the Government claimed the meteorites were made of radioactive material, which produced a grand chemical reaction when heated with the earth's gravitational pull. The reaction emitted unknown agents into the environment. Although not all side effects were known, scientists were working on it, or so the TV reporter said.

"But obvious effects from the chemical reaction have been identified," the news anchor continued. "When the meteorites exploded, they released a still unidentified agent that caused anyone exposed to it to fall into deep unconsciousness for about twenty-four hours. Another airborne agent has apparently embedded itself in the human body." The woman paused as she cupped her hand around her ear. "I'm just receiving word that they are calling the airborne agent ATHENS."

Appearing at the bottom of the screen were the words: ATHENS: **A**erosolized **Th**ymine **E**nervating **N**anoparticle**s**. The words faded within less than a heartbeat, with no time to study them.

Lana let out a snorting laugh.

"It's not funny," Isabel scolded. "Why are you laughing?"

"Because they're not telling us anything. They're just giving this tiny meteor dust a meaningless science-y name," Lana replied.

Isabel stood, rolled her eyes at Cory, then went into her room and slammed the door behind her.

"Why did you have to piss her off?" Cory said, looking at Lana. "But you're right. The Government doesn't know what that dust is, or what it does. They just act like they do."

Lana had been starring at her laptop, and when she responded, it was through clenched teeth.

"Whatever it is, it's spreading everywhere. We're breathing it in. And if these guys are right," she tapped the screen, "it might even be affecting us at a cellular level." Seeing Cory's confused face, she added, "It might change or affect our DNA, and even our nervous systems."

Lana then suggested to Cory that they gather as much food and water as possible. If this was the beginning of the end of the world, they wanted to be prepared for it. If they pooled their resources, they could buy enough supplies to last them at least through a year if they rationed it right.

The next day, Cory and Isabel went to file a missing person's report, but returned home angry. After hours of waiting, they were handed sheets to fill out and told to mail them to a regional center being set up for missing persons. Neither of them believed the police could help find their mother.

Lana finally contacted her grandmother, who was packing to move to the inner city where Giovanni said they would be protected. Her grandmother insisted she come stay with her, and wanted to arrange a charter flight to pick her up, but Lana thanked her and refused. For now at least, she would stay with Cory and Isabel.

A week later, Cory's mother still had not returned, and Isabel's emails and calls to the regional center went unanswered. The Government had promised answers, but people were losing faith in the Government's ability to handle the crisis. It didn't take long before folks ignored the authority's warnings to stay indoors and wait for the dust to settle down.

Political leaders appeared on television to announce the world's food and water supplies had been contaminated, and the consumption of contaminated foods would cause internal damage. To avoid unimaginable pain, people were advised to throw away all food and water supplies that weren't verified by the Government. Furthermore, the World Government declared, they had secured a limited amount of uncontaminated food and water, and actions were being taken to replace the contaminated supplies with these.

The majority of the world's population took heed of the warnings and tossed away any supplies that the Government hadn't verified. However, the price of food and water rose to a point where low-income earners could no longer afford to feed their families; even middle-class families found it difficult to provide the basic necessities for their homes. Looting and riots increased.

The Government pleaded with people to move to the new regional food distribution centers. Many left for the camps, never to return. Companies closed down, and the majority of jobs left were government jobs. The world plummeted into great depression, and with no stable economy, combined with the lack of food and water, crime rates rose overnight.

With the substantial rise in crime, the Government nationalized the food and water industry and deployed armed militia to safeguard their resources.

Weeks turned into months. Things had deteriorated so much that larger cities were placed under martial law. That's the time the major effects of ATHENS began to show.

The death rate dropped to almost zero. ATHENS had rendered humans immune to death. Everybody on the planet appeared to have become immortal. Even animals were affected.

It did not, however, affect immunity to disease and pain. Any illness people had before The Sabbath, continued to torment them after it. Even more shocking, ATHENS seemed to have increased the amount of time the human body needed to heal. The symptoms of illness and pain increased ten fold. If a person got a simple cut, it felt like a razor-sharp blade being pierced into his skin. If he caught a simple cold, it felt like a high fever until his body had healed.

Childbirth was ATHENS' biggest irony. It did a wonderful job of sustaining life, but made the human body toxic. Almost all pregnancies resulted in miscarriage.

With no offspring, the world became a dark and gloomy place. The thought of living forever once brought joy to people's hearts, over time it became clear that ATHENS was a curse destroying the very essence of humanity.

The passing of months turned into a year since the night of the Sabbath. The only businesses still operational were government agencies and a few corporations. Financial and commercial transactions continued to be available, but only for the very rich. Surprisingly, electricity and communications remained intact, for the most part. The corruption of Government officials was also at an all-time high. At the right price, police officers could be bought at ease and persuaded to do whatever was needed of them. There weren't enough prison cells to detain everyone, let alone resources to feed them, and the Government was desperately trying to come up with a solution. Hospitals were crowded with patients without insurance, so doctors did only the bare minimum. They would patch them up then send them back onto the streets to fend for themselves.

The world Cory and Lana knew was no longer. ATHENS turned society into a two-class system: the elites and the "others." While Cory's neighbors made an exodus to the south for warmer weather, the elites migrated into the inner city under the protection of armed militia. Government agencies began building walls and barricading the entrance for the others. Cory and Lana never got access to the inner city, but from what Lana's grandmother told them, the rich lived as they always did. Nothing had changed.

"Hi, Grandma," Lana said, gazing out the window.

"Hey, baby. I was hoping you'd call. How are you?"

Lana gripped the phone and murmured to herself.

"Huh," her grandmother's voice rang. "Lana, is everything all right?"

"Sorry, Grandma," Lana said, reverting her attention back to her phone call. "I just saw two guys outside robbing this homeless old man."

"Good lord. Call the police."

Lana put her hand to her forehead, and let out a small laugh. She had been careful, up to now, to pretend she was living a normal life when talking with her grandmother. Too late to take it back now. Lana took a deep breath, resigned to her grandmother's predictable reaction.

"Grandma, around here the police and the thugs are the same people."

"That's awful. Lana, what kind of place are you living?"

"Same place, just on the opposite side of the wall," Lana answered.

Lana and the rest of the others lived in the trenches. Outside the inner cities, you were on your own. How far out you lived from the inner city determined the amount of public services you received from the Government. Cory's house was just on the outskirts and the only public service Lana ever saw was a garbage truck driving through their neighborhood and a few corrupt police officers.

"Anyways, Grandma, tell me about what's happening in the inner city."

"Nothing really. They just reopened the schools."

"Schools? You guys are getting schools?" Mounting frustration crept into Lana's voice.

"Yes, aren't you?" her grandmother asked.

"No," Lana barked. "My gosh, wake up."

"Lana," her grandmother shrieked.

"Sorry, Grandma. I've got to go. I'll call you later."

Lana hung up without waiting for a response. Her grandmother's ignorance annoyed her beyond belief, but it wasn't her grandmother's fault. The Government went to great length to ensure the inner city was disconnected from the outside world. Of course, Lana could fly out to be with her grandmother, but she wouldn't leave Cory. The chaos brought out a consolation prize: Love.

And Cory was devoted to her. Lana and Isabel were his world, and every decision he made was for the girls' survival. With no job or schooling, they had to be resourceful. Their home was their first project.

The house had a storm cellar, which they dedicated for supply stock. One room was lined with deep freezers, and the other resembled a grocery, hardware and appliance store all in one. Their weapons were also kept in there. For security, they built a wall-to-wall bookshelf to conceal the cellar's entrance and updated the security of their home to reduce the possibility of break-ins and to maintain their safety.

They also made their own greywater recycling system so waste water from the bath, shower or sink, was collected into two soil pipes fixed to the side of the house, then pumped up into the loft to be stored in a tank. The water could then be filtered and reused.

As more time went by, food and water became even scarcer. Government trucks were always being raided for supplies. With no future income, it wasn't long before Cory convinced both Lana and Isabel that they needed to join in on the raids.

At first, Cory went alone and did the same as everyone else, running toward the armed trucks, while at the same time competing with other raiders for limited resources.

Then, they got smarter - Lana called and persuaded her grandmother to arrange funds, which they used to bribe a man in charge of protecting the convoys. After that, during raids, Cory and Lana waited for the first and second wave of looters to hit the truck. Then, amidst the chaos, they headed for the designated rendezvous point to meet their confidant and retrieve their supplies.

The man often showed a fondness toward Lana, so Cory's eyes never wavered from his sight, even though the guy had proven time and time again that he was trustworthy in other ways. Routinely, they stole food, appliances, solar-powered tools and such. They were prepared for anything and everything.

5

"Good morning," Lana greeted a half-asleep Isabel as she walked into the kitchen.

"Good morning," Isabel replied with a shy smile before returning to her room.

It had been over a year, and Isabel still blamed herself for her mother's disappearance. She tried to avoid Lana and Cory when she was at home and mostly, she was never home. She left the house before they woke up on most days and came home after they went to sleep.

Lana wished she could help her, but Cory hadn't made it easy for either of them; there was so much tension in the household. Although he had apologized for attacking Isabel, every day their mother was missing, another layer of tension and blame grew between the siblings.

Lana shook her head, not wanting to think about it anymore, and removed a bowl and spoon from the cupboard. She slept without eating dinner last night and woke up to a growling stomach. She poured herself her favorite cereal with milk, and instead of watching the news and hearing the same-old story about The Sabbath, she called her grandmother. Grabbing her phone, she dialed the number she knew so well.

"Hello, darling, why are you awake so early?" her grandmother asked, sounding preoccupied.

"I went to sleep hungry last night, and my stomach woke me up...what are you *doing*?" Lana snapped. It always annoyed her when her grandmother didn't give her undivided attention during their phone calls.

"Oh, relax darling," her grandmother was used to this, "I'm just doing my morning stretches. With all this disease in the world, I need to stay healthy - not only for me, but also for you - not to mention I need to keep these middle-aged women in check. Anyways, you sound like something is bothering you. What's wrong?"

Lana hesitated, not wanting to complain to her grandmother. She wanted her grandmother to deem her a brave young woman, but she needed someone to confide in -someone who supported her and gave her the advice she needed.

"Lana?" her grandmother called, uncertain if she was still on the phone.

"I'm still here. I have no idea where to start."

"Anywhere, honey," her grandmother said.

"Okay…well," the words rushed out, "Cory's mom is still missing - it's been over a year, and she is just nowhere to be found. She's sick, but she can't die, so, that means she might still be in excruciating pain, and her family wouldn't know where."

She took a breath before she collapsed.

"I can't even talk to Cory about it. It's like she's a forbidden topic in the house, and it's getting on my nerves. It's frustrating, but she's not the only one missing. So many other people's family members are missing. We need to try and figure this thing out. We're smart people, but we're at a standstill.

"What needs to happen now?" her grandmother asked, encouraging her thoughts just as she had done when Lana was a child.

"I want to figure out what's going on - why people can't die, why people are missing…why the whole world has stopped, and society has fallen apart. Everyone is living for themselves. No one works; no one does anything at all.

"I'm not buying that the explosion in the sky caused all of this. Grandma, something else is going on - and Cory would see it too, if he just took a second and stopped blaming Isabel for their mother's disappearance. We're more than capable of finding her if we put our university-educated, critical minded selves to work and not be like the masses who have fallen into the routine of this new life."

As Lana finished, she felt relief that she could explain this to someone who didn't shut her down by saying they have more important things to worry about.

"You're smart, and you can find the inconsistencies in the stories that the Government has been giving us. And as for Cory - you have to appeal to him in a way he will be willing to listen, and be able to respond to you in the manner you need. You're more than capable of doing that; that's one of your many talents. Honey, don't let this situation overwhelm you. Don't lose yourself in all this. You're stronger than that," her grandmother finished her lecture-come-motivational speech.

"Okay. Thanks, Grandma. I'll figure it out," Lana said, relieved, and now with a renewed sense of hope.

"Lana, there's one more thing. I know I say this every time we talk, but sweetheart, you can always come home and live with Giovanni and me. I would sleep so much better knowing you're safe. His place is plenty safe, and you wouldn't have to worry about food or anything…" her grandmother paused, waiting for a response.

"I know, and I appreciate it Gram - I really do. But Cory needs me here. Besides, who else will keep those two from killing each other? I promise at the first sign of real danger, I will be right there to live with you and Giovanni."

Lana always said that to her grandmother when she brought up the topic of her coming to live with them. She loved her grandmother, and even Giovanni had grown on her over the past year; even so, she couldn't bring herself to leave Cory. Although she had come close to leaving quite often, following arguments between all three of them, she never did.

"I'll call you tomorrow, Grandma. Be safe."

"Love you, darling."

Lana hung up the phone and sat back in her chair. She took a deep breath, still trying to figure out what she would say to Cory when he returned home. She finished her breakfast and then grabbed the trash bag from the kitchen before stepping out of the house.

Lana's mind continued to race.

If we can do all this, why can't we figure out what's going on and where all the missing people are? Okay, what should I say to Cory to get him to help me?

One, the Government hasn't even addressed the missing people.

Two, why is the water still contaminated?

People just don't disappear like that. The Government must know something. I need to find a connection there. Once I find the connection, I'll think Cory would…

A strong male voice interrupted her thoughts.

"…I tell you! They're liars! They are paid to deceive and to hide the truth amongst lies. The Government is not to be trusted—they are to blame for *all* your problems!" shouted an old man at the end of the street.

He was tall, about 6'2", with a frighteningly pale complexion, a balding hairline and a full gray beard. Dressed like a bum, he wore tattered clothing and carried a huge camping bag around with him everywhere he went. He spoke with an accent that Lana could not place, but she narrowed it down to South America.

It had surprised her that he was well spoken and quite smart. Lana never understood why he was ranting about political ideologies instead of quietly trying to survive like everyone else. He was always hanging around Cory's neighborhood, shouting to anyone willing to acknowledge his presence.

Come to think of it, he had been around ever since Lana had met Cory four years ago. In a way, he was their neighbor, but homeless as far as she could tell. At first, Lana had assumed he was crazy, but considering their current situation, he might not have been as offset as she had thought.

Yeah, man, I agree. They are liars!

Lana threw the garbage into a large dumpster and walked back to Cory's yard. She slid her thumb over the sensor by the door and unlocked it, then entered the house, but not before glancing back once more at the old man shouting down the street.

His gaze caught hers, and Lana felt as if he had heard her agree with him. She pulled her eyes away and the door closed behind her, locking automatically.

Lana shivered as she walked into the living room. *That encounter was so odd.* She checked on their surveillance system while she waited for Cory to get home.

Lana was always interested in computers and science. Although there were not a lot of women in her field of chemical engineering, she had always dominated and outshone everyone else in her classes. When The Sabbath hit and violence grew, she used her time to rewire the home alarm devices with some highly classified technology she had gotten from Doug during a raid. Doug, their confidant with the Government, had a crush on her, and she used it to her advantage. He helped her get big company technologies - items like finger sensor locks, bullet-proof film material, small cameras for video surveillance, and sound proofing equipment.

Lana collected gadgets at every opportunity and altered their original functions to protect Cory's house, her new home. She ensured that the windows and the exterior walls were bullet and soundproof. The doors opened and closed automatically, but only with Cory's, Isabel's or her fingerprints.

She had turned the house into a bunker. No one entered without proper identification; no stray bullets could cause injuries. To keep people from noticing the technological home they had developed, she ensured the exterior of the house remained the same as it was always had been, raising little suspicion.

Although Lana hated the situation making this necessary, she enjoyed the unique opportunity it gave her to explore her talents and capabilities. She had never known she was so inclined to technology and had the abilities to create such things. The house became a pet project of hers, and one she was more than proud of.

It also provided an escape for her when the tension between the three of them became unbearable.

Instead of focusing on the surveillance tape, Lana found herself uneasy. She decided to watch television, hoping that it would take her mind off her anticipated talk with Cory. Instead, she dozed off halfway through a show.

6

When Cory came home, he found Lana lying on the living room sofa. He stood and marveled at the sight. Cory could watch her sleep all day. Lana was his rib, and Cory cared for her deeply. But she scared him.

Living outside the inner city was a struggle, something that Lana did not have to endure. With one phone call, she could leave at any moment, and the thought tormented Cory.

To cushion the blow if it were to happen, Cory kept his feelings hidden. But his insecurities were beginning to take its toll as Lana pleaded for him to connect and express himself. Cory wished he could, but every time he tried, he panicked. He didn't want to burden Lana with his problems, and he feared giving Lana his all when she could walk out on him.

What happened to 'I can't sleep unless you're by my side,' he joked, pulling the remote away from Lana's hand and turning off the TV. He walked to Isabel's room, and while clutching the doorknob with his right hand, he knocked.

"Bell, you in there?" he yelled.

"Yeahhh…"

Pushing the door open, he found Isabel in bed wrapped up in her blanket.

"Hey, are you all right?" he asked.

"Yeah, just a bit under the weather," she replied.

It always shocked Cory when people got sick now, when it was all but impossible for them to die. He remembered the first time he caught a cold after The Sabbath and how within two hours it turned into a high fever. It was the worst fever he'd ever had. His body temperature spiked up to 106 degrees Fahrenheit. It was like being engulfed with flames. To make matters worse, he had little energy to eat, spending most of his time in and out of consciousness. He shrugged off the horrible memory.

"Get some rest. I'll be back to bring you some medicine."

He headed into the kitchen and scanned the top of the refrigerator where they kept their medication. Grabbing a bottle of Tylenol, he took out six tablets, blatantly ignoring the bottle's clear instructions of only taking two. He poured a cup of water into a glass, careful not to spill a single precious drop, and walked back into Isabel's room.

"Here, take this," he said, handing Isabel the drink and the medication. Cory waited until Isabel swallowed each pill before leaving her room.

I need some fresh air.

He walked to the living room window and poked his upper body out. He closed his eyes for a few seconds and sighed, embracing the warm breeze. It was a quiet spring night, no later than eight o'clock. Nights like this reminded him how things had been before The Sabbath. Turning his head, he scouted the area for any activity.

He noticed the familiar old man packing up his things as if he was going home. *That crazy old man is still out there.* Long before the meteorites, Cory had his fair share of interactions with the man. Every day as Cory left for school, the old man would be there on the corner, talking what sounded like pure nonsense. Cory would do his best to ignore him, but sometimes he rudely insisted the old-timer leave him alone. Cory's mother, on the other hand, would entertain the old man and his foolishness. He remembered arguing with his mother about why she chose to enable his craziness. Cory chuckled at the memory.

"Babe..." Lana's voice called from behind.

He turned to the sight of her stretching her arms and yawning. He laughed before saying, "Jeez, sleeping beauty has awoken!"

Lana squinted her eyes and gave Cory a scornful look before deciding she would not go there just then, "Anyways, did you find something?"

"No," Cory replied, disappointment evident in his voice.

Cory had been gone all day looking for work. The raids were becoming too dangerous, and he wanted to find another way to support them. The problem was the jobs available had a long list of candidates, and since his school closed right after The Sabbath, he wasn't even qualified enough to be considered for the few government jobs left.

"Don't worry, you'll figure something out," Lana said, trying to cheer him up.

Cory nodded and walked toward the kitchen. Judging by his mood, Lana wasn't sure if she should still talk to him about the things that had been bothering her all day. But she couldn't hold it in any longer.

"Cory…umm…we need to talk," she said.

"Yeah, wassup?" he replied.

"Well, it's been over a year, and we haven't got any answer to what's going on."

"Yeah, so what do you want me to do about it?"

"I'm just saying - I feel like we should start looking into it ourselves."

"Looking into what, the missing people?"

"Yes."

"Lana, not again," Cory rolled his head. "We've talked about this."

"Well, we need to talk about it again," Lana said.

"Okay. Talk."

"Fine. I don't think we did enough to find your mother."

Cory chuckled.

"Lana, I think those naps have been messing with your head. You don't remember those nights I didn't sleep because I was out there looking for her? Or how I was gone for so long that you thought I went missing too?"

"Yes, I remember, but-"

"But what?" Cory interrupted, slapping his hand on the kitchen counter. "What do you want me to do? Lana, I spent months looking for her. It wasn't easy, but I came to terms that she was gone. Why are you trying to make me relive it?"

Lana took a calming breath.

"Cory, I know the pain you went through, but we got to try again. I don't want to wake up every day doing the same ol' things, hoping one day, the Government will finally tell us the truth," Lana said, raising her voice.

Cory sensed her mounting frustration and wasn't in any mood to argue, so he tried reasoning with her, "Babe, you're right, but just like last time, we don't know where to start. So how are we supposed to find answers without the slightest clue as to where to look, huh?"

"It'll be different this time. Look at everything we've accomplished. We can get the resources to find her."

Cory clapped his hands. "Lana, I'm done talking about this."

"Well, I'm not. People just don't disappear into thin air, and last time I checked, there wasn't an alien abduction in the news. So where are they?"

Cory stayed quiet. He planned on letting Lana vent for a bit, hoping she would soon calm down. But his silence heightened her frustration.

She shook her head.

"God, it's like you don't even care! You wake up doing the same things every day for nothing. All this shit you're doing…you forget your mom hasn't come home yet. Like, where's your mom, Cory, where is she?"

Cory clenched his jaw as veins erupted on his forehead.

"Are you saying I don't notice my mom not being here?" Cory said in a low, but stern voice.

Lana grabbed the edge of shirt and twirled it between her fingers. She tilted her head down, staring at the hardwood but did not say a word.

Her silence heightened his frustration.

"Lana?" Cory shouted.

Lana looked up to Cory with his jaw still clenched and glaring eyes.

"No," she barked. "No- I mean yes. It does feel like you forgotten. Why am I even begging you to look for your own mother? You're not doing anything to find her."

"Man, fuck you," Cory lashed back.

Lana's lips started quivering and she couldn't blink fast enough to keep the tears from escaping.

"Her room has not changed since she left," Cory continued with his finger pointing at the stairs. "While you have your rich Grandma you can call at any time. I'm out here busting my ass for you so you can still take your stupid afternoon naps. And now you're trying to tell me I'm not doing enough? Don't fucking pretend to know how I feel. I haven't been able to sleep since she left. So *fuck-*"

She slapped him.

In complete despair, Lana cupped her face in her hands, blocking away the tears and ran past Cory. He was the only one who managed to get the better of her; now that his voice carried so much hatred and anger, it was too much for her to bear. There was a deep sense of numbness in the pit of her stomach.

Meanwhile, Cory just stood there in awe: mouth wide open and rubbing his jaw. The place went silent until he heard a *click* - the sound of his bedroom door locking.

He was unsure of what to do next. The damage was done, but he was too proud to console Lana, regardless of how much it killed him watching her cry.

"I don't need this," he said to himself.

He paced back and forth, pondering how everything had escalated so fast. At times like this, he would call his boys, but The Sabbath made it nearly impossible to stay in contact. He had no one to turn to.

I shouldn't have told her off, but she was asking for it. Saying those things about my mom and then having the nerve to cry... was I in the right? Lost in his thoughts, Cory realized that Lana was right. As time passed, it became easier for him to block out his mother's disappearance from his mind.

He pulled out his wallet and took out an old picture of his mother smiling. *Why did I stop looking for her?* Cory knew the answer though - he allowed himself to believe his responsibilities as a man kept him from searching for his mother. He had to make sure they had everything they needed in case of another disaster. But in actuality, he was afraid of what he might find. He had just learnt to accept his mother's disappearance. He wasn't ready to accept something worse happening to his mother.

He shook his head trying to free his mind, but it kept haunting him. *Where do I even look? And won't the Government bring her back.*

Cory didn't believe the Government would ensure his mother's safe return, but it was the only thing he could come up with to keep him from feeling like a terrible son. To avoid going deeper into his thoughts, he reverted his attention back to Lana and how he would fix things between them. Giving her time to cool off was the only way Cory knew how to handle Lana's outburst, and he prayed this situation wouldn't be any different.

He stopped pacing, to open the fridge and count their food supplies. It was enough to last a complete month before they had to go into their cellar to get more. He made himself a quick bite to eat, then stretched out on the living room sofa. The fight came at a horrible time; he was exhausted and wanted nothing more than to sink into his bed, but Lana would much rather slap him in the face than open the bedroom door for him. Cory considered sleeping in his mother's room, but he feared that it would be too much to bear.

Ain't this some shit? I have a comfortable bed, but I'm sleeping on the couch! What a wonderful girlfriend she is.

7

Lana awoke the next morning, still bitter about the night before.

Ugh, he's so dumb, she thought as she lay in bed, staring up at the ceiling.

Eventually, she got up and stumbled into the bathroom. She grabbed a bucket of dirty water on the floor and carried it to the kitchen. Glancing out into the living room, she saw Cory was still sleeping a few feet away. Not prepared for any interactions with him, she hurried to get her bath water ready.

Setting the bucket on the counter and grabbing a strainer and a large pot from the cabinet, she placed the pot on the stove and poured the dirty water into it. Next, she turned the heat on high and leaned against the counter, waiting for the water to boil.

Asshole, Lana thought, watching as Cory stirred on the sofa.

After fifteen minutes, the water appeared much cleaner. She poured it back into the bucket, letting it pass through the strainer before tiptoeing back into the bathroom.

Once there, she filled an empty cup with a little water from the bucket and brushed her teeth over the sink, careful not to waste any water. She removed her clothes and took the cup and the bucket of water into the bathtub with her.

Standing close to the bucket, she dipped the cup into the water. Stretching her other arm so that her hand and fingertips dangled over the bucket, she poured the water over her head. The water ran off her head, over her shoulder, down her arm and back into the bucket.

Setting the cup aside, she grabbed a clean washcloth from the railing and dunked it in the water. To keep the bucket of water as clean as possible, she stepped back to scrub her body with soap.

"What a jerk," she said absentmindedly.

Grabbing the cup, she rinsed herself until she was clean. *Oh there's still some water left.* Taking the bucket from the tub, she set it aside for the next person.

Lana hoped taking a bath would help clear her mind, but all she kept thinking of were the many ways she planned on ignoring her boyfriend. She stared at herself in the mirror, contemplating whether she should have taken her grandmother's advice and gone home.

As often as she had tried to get through to Cory, she always got shut down. But this time it was different. It wasn't what Cory said that had made Lana upset, but it was the way he'd said it. The hatred in his eyes...the anger in his voice seemed almost identical to the time when he had lashed out at Isabel. Keeping his emotions bottled up on the inside was poisonous to their relationship, and Lana wasn't sure if she could go through that scenario again. Wrapping herself up in a white towel, she walked back into his room and locked the door.

Once dressed, Lana sat on the bed and pondered calling her grandmother, but she already anticipated what she would say. *Maybe she's right; the only person who ever got through his stubbornness is missing, so there isn't much I can do anymore...yeah, Grandma is right, it's time for me to go home...there's nothing here for me anymore.*

Jumping up and grabbing all of her clothes from the closet, she tossed them onto the bed and went back to the closet for her suitcase. *Gotta call Grandma to arrange my travel back home,* she thought while stuffing her luggage with clothes. Lana had her mind fixed on leaving Cory this time and wanted to do it quickly, before anyone or anything convinced her otherwise.

As hard as it may have been, Lana had lost hope. Perhaps there were some things even love could not overcome? Even though they were not on good terms, Lana realized she had to figure out a way to break the news to Cory without him persuading her to stay. But before she could think, there came a knock on the door.

It was him.

"No matter what, no matter what, you're leaving!" she declared to herself in preparation for her final talk with Cory.

An awkward tension greeted the two as soon as Lana opened the door.

Although Cory had no problem stirring up trouble, figuring out how to solve it was never his strong suit. It was hard for him to express his feelings because he was always afraid of putting himself in a position to be hurt. Yet, Lana hated when Cory remained aloof, since she always told him everything going on with her.

Cory understood he could not fix things with Lana without communicating his feelings, and he prepared himself to give her the bare minimum. He had stayed up all night planning on what to say, but when he saw Lana's blank face, he froze. Cory cracked a grin; he figured his charm would win her over.

Is this guy serious? she thought.

"There's nothing funny, Cory," she sneered.

Cory straightened his lips, removing his smirk.

"Sorry, I know…Baby, can we talk?"

"We talked yesterday. Remember?" Lana scolded, turning away and walking toward the bed.

Cory followed and stopped short when he saw Lana's clothes and open suitcase spread out on his bed. Glaring at his closet, he noticed she had taken all of her belongings. If she were to leave, it would be for good. He stood still as Lana continued packing.

"What are you doing?" he asked not moving a muscle. Cory already knew the answer, but he wanted her to say it.

Lana stopped to stare at Cory. His face showed more confusion than anger, and she'd expected as much. Lana had been living with them for over a year now, and after all the fights they'd had in the past, she had not once acted on her thoughts of leaving him.

Tell him you're leaving. She opened her mouth, but words wouldn't come out. This would be harder than she imagined. She couldn't bring herself to tell him, so she ignored him and continued packing.

"Why?" Cory choked, "Why are you doing this?"

Putting her head down, she avoided any eye contact because she would as usual gravitate toward him and that was the last thing she needed. *Stay strong; stay strong,* she repeated to herself.

Tilting his head toward the ceiling, Cory puffed his cheeks full of air and blew out his frustration.

"So you're leaving me?"

Bothered greatly by Lana ignoring him, Cory walked over to where she stood packing and pressed his face in front of hers.

"You're really leaving, Lana?" he implored.

Lana brushed him aside and moved to the other side of the bed. She saw the hurt in his eyes and how much her pending departure was destroying him.

"Cory...stop. Don't make this harder than it already is," she finally blurted, fighting back tears.

He blinked at Lana; he couldn't understand why she was doing this. The fight last night was nothing compared to what they'd been through together. Straightening his back, Cory nodded then sucked his teeth.

"Cool, cool, cool. All right - let me help you pack."

He snatched her clothes and started stuffing them into her suitcase.

Lana grabbed his arms, "Stop! You're ruining my clothes!"

Cory shook off her grip. He grabbed the suitcase with both hands and hurled it across the room. The luggage hit the wall with a thud, leaving behind a trail of clothes.

Lana jumped in his face, screaming, "What the fuck is wrong with you? Don't act like you care now."

A large lump crept up in the back of her throat as her eyes watered.

Cory was also on the verge of tears. But he refused to cry over a female who wasn't his mother, no matter how much it hurt him. Tilting his head toward the ceiling, he fought off the tears as his pride took over.

I'm not gonna beg no girl to stay, I don't need her...never did. No matter how many times he tried to convince himself he didn't need Lana, he knew letting her go was a mistake, but he had no way of making her stay. And it was way past the point of apologizing.

Turning his back to Lana, Cory plodded to the wall. *It's happening all over again*, he thought. With tears streaming down his face, he pounded the wall with his knuckles until blood dripped from his hand. He needed to feel physical pain to release the colossal emotional hurt he was experiencing. Like a madman, he strode to the door and swung it open; there was a loud thud as the door contacted the wall.

"Fine, leave! I don't need you, Lana. You wouldn't be the first person to walk out on me. My dad, my mom, my friends,...now you're going to leave me, too! I've been through it - I don't need you! I'm good all by myself. Leave!" Cory charged out of the room, leaving Lana inside.

Lana stood motionless, processing what just had happened. It was the first time Cory mentioned his father, and it surprised her. She was so stunned she forgot about leaving. Although she was sure that Cory's mother didn't leave him, at least not by choice, his dad was a whole other story - a story Lana had never heard and didn't expect to.

Why was he crying? Should I leave? He told me to leave. I should leave; he doesn't treat me like he wants me. No matter how hard I try, I still just make him upset. Anger is about the only emotion he knows how to express. Ugh, he's such an asshole.

Frustration, anger, and hurt easing its way back into her consciousness. With moist eyes, her mind played back all the smart-ass comments Cory made about her sleeping, eating, or not doing anything at all. This was his fault anyway—or so she thought. She wanted to call her grandmother, but it wasn't a good idea. The last thing Lana needed was to give her grandmother any reason to dislike her boyfriend. For now, she would just have to deal with this all by herself.

Not ready to leave Cory's room, she cleaned up the mess Cory had made of her clothes. The luggage was broke. The handle had fallen off and the zipper was jagged and torn, now unable to close. Feeling defeated, she let out a huge sigh and sat on the floor. This was not how she imagined things would have ended. Closing her eyes and sighing, her head tilted back. Not having the strength to leave anymore, she just sat on the floor, back against the wall, staring at the hole Cory had just punched in.

What do I do now?

8

Cory stormed out of the house, dripping blood with his every stride.

This is so fucking ridiculous! She's so fucking annoying. She can go; I don't need her.

He got into his car and sat still. Feeling crushed, he wanted to drive as far from the house as possible. But with nowhere to go, he stayed parked in his driveway, monitoring the activities of his neighbors and hoping that it would take his mind off things.

He paid little attention to the few people out and about. His affections toward Lana still consumed him, and the throbbing pain in his hand made no difference either.

After several minutes, the cool morning air had calmed him, but he still continued to convince himself that Lana wasn't needed. In reality, though, he wouldn't be able to survive without Lana.

It wasn't just his love for her, but if not for Lana's modifications to their home, he wouldn't have electricity, let alone their inventory in the cellar. Deep down inside, in a place kept hidden from his pride, he realized that he needed Lana more than she needed him.

Buried in his thoughts, he reminisced about the first time the two met.

***

It had been during his first year of university. It was exam season. Cory had just finished classes for the day and had been on his way to the library to meet his friend, so they could study together.

They were standing in the middle of the library, scanning for a vacant spot, when his friend tugged his arm. Cory turned toward where his friend was pointing and noticed a woman sitting at a desk. Her head buried in her books.

"Yo, who is that?" he whispered.

Cory squinted to get a better visual, and saw Lana's soft caramel complexion and a body that other women would kill for. Before Cory could answer, his friend was already striding toward her. He was either bold or stupid, but one thing was for sure, Cory wanted to see how things played out. While standing in the background, he watched his friend's flimsy attempt to impress Lana with outlandish compliments. To Cory's surprise, interrupting Lana from studying didn't upset her, and she even entertained his shenanigans.

Judging by her body language, Cory recognized Lana wasn't interested, and was just being polite, so he didn't bother saying much during their first encounter. Afterwards, every time Cory would cross paths with Lana, they would exchange hellos before going about their business.

It wasn't until the second semester, when Cory and Lana shared the same class, that they had their first real conversation. After a couple of assignments together, they exchanged contact information, and from there, their relationship grew as the year progressed.

***

Cory smirked at the memory. Back then, Lana's beauty attracted many men - and she often used it to her advantage, but in this present time, it was much better to stay under the radar. Cory would never forget the first time Lana had been in danger.

***

On a warm afternoon, after The Sabbath, Cory had gone out for a run and returned to find music blaring from his home. It sounded like a party, and that was the last thing they needed.

He approached his house with caution, and when he opened the door, he saw Isabel lying on the floor with a black eye and a swollen jaw. The house appeared as if a tornado had blown through the place. He kneeled down to check on Isabel. She was unconscious as he picked her up and laid her on the couch. The sight of Isabel's fragile state made Cory furious, whilst at the same time; guilty that he wasn't there to stop it.

***

That must have been how she felt when I blamed her for mom. Shrugging off the guilt, he jumped back into the memory.

***

He turned off the music and heard Lana's terrified screams coming

36

from Isabel's room. Stopping to grab a knife from the kitchen, he found the door was locked, so he rammed it open. His anxiety spiked ten fold as he saw Lana lying on the bed, restrained by a half-naked man, her knees up against her chest trying to kick him away. The man was much bigger than Cory, but that didn't matter. Adrenaline took over, and later on, all he remembered was being on top of the pervert, stabbing him in the chest, not stopping until Lana and Isabel pulled him off.

He regained his composure as he stood over the culprit's unresponsive body. Covered in blood, Cory wanted to hurt the dirt-bag even more, but the man was already out cold. He wouldn't die, but with this much damage done, it would be months - if not years, before he healed or regained consciousness.

Once everyone had calmed down, they called the police then waited two long hours for them to arrive to carry the culprit away on a stretcher.

The defiler never got a chance to rape Lana, but ever since that day, they modified their home to be a haven from intruders. Cory now always called or texted every thirty minutes whenever he left the house, just to make sure everything was all right.

If Lana left, he wouldn't be able to watch over her anymore. Cory took comfort in the thought he could protect Lana in a way that her grandmother and step-grandfather couldn't.

***

His contentment faded in a flash as an old man walking past his car interrupted his thoughts. He had on a dirty white t-shirt and torn blue jeans. Judging by his appearance, the geezer was homeless. But he never begged for change. Instead, he always ranted about an upcoming apocalypse.

Oh, this guy again! I wonder what's he's preaching about now?

And for the first time, Cory was intrigued. The old man had been ranting on this same street corner since Cory was little. And with everyone acting crazy, Cory realized this was the same old man he used to bicker with his mother about, and was the one person he knew that hadn't changed since The Sabbath.

Hey, there must have been a reason why mom would entertain him.

Cory got out of his car and approached the man.

"Hey, what are you talking about?" he asked.

The old man ignored him and kept chanting, "Lies. They're all lies!"

Cory couldn't blame the old-timer for disregarding him. He had said some pretty rude things to him in the past, and now he appeared to be receiving the backlash of it.

Cory grabbed him by the arm, "Yo, please. Tell me."

The old man looked at Cory and recognized the desperation written on his face. He pointed to Cory's house and said, "All right, let's go inside."

Cory wasn't sure if it was wise to bring a homeless man into his state-of-the-art home, but he agreed to it anyway. The old man didn't intimidate him at all. He sat the old-timer at the dining room table. Isabel and Lana were nowhere to be found when they entered.

However, Lana walked out of Cory's room after hearing an unfamiliar voice. She was shocked to find Cory sitting with the old man from the corner, the one who may or may not have read her thoughts that same day. Ever since The Sabbath, they had kept to themselves and had never once invited a guest over.

What is he doing here? Lana was still upset at Cory. Instead of asking him what he was thinking by bringing a stranger inside their home, she made herself comfortable on the living room couch. She sat just far enough so that Cory's presence wouldn't annoy her, but close enough to listen to everything being said.

"How do y'all get yo electricity?" he asked.

"The sun," Cory answered. "It's all solar power."

The old man nodded in approval.

"Give me a glass of water," he demanded with a straight face.

Cory raised his eyebrows in astonishment. He wasn't sure if he had heard him right, "Huh?"

"Give me a glass of water, son," the old man repeated.

Cory stared at him for a few seconds. *This motherfucker is asking for water...like it's free. Like it doesn't cost fifty dollars a gallon. He really must be crazy.*

Turning to Lana, Cory saw she was just as stunned. He looked back to the old man.

While nodding his head, the man clapped his hands.

"Okay," Cory replied, getting up and walking toward the kitchen. There was one jug of water left in the refrigerator.

Okay, everybody is supposed to get two cups of water daily, so I guess he can have one of mine...but it's not too late to kick him out though. Cory was regretting inviting him over, but his curiosity prevented Cory from giving him the old heave-ho just yet. Grabbing a glass from the cabinet, he poured.

"More," the old man boomed when he saw Cory had filled the glass halfway.

Cory gave him a look and continued pouring.

"That's your fraction," Lana grumbled.

Cory ignored her and handed the old man the water. To their surprise, he didn't devour the water like a thirsty man as they had both expected. Instead he took the glass and drank the water with grace, as if he himself had an abundant supply. With a grin on his face, he sat back on his chair and said, "The truth isn't cheap, son."

The old man enjoyed testing Cory's patience. He asked Cory to sit down before continuing their conversation.

"I'm sorry about what happened to yo momma. She was a good woman - I saw her face in you …God knows she's the only reason I am sitting down with you right now, son. Look at how the world is today! We've tried to warn y'all for decades now, but y'all wouldn't listen.

"The Government strips us of our clothes and homes, drugs us, and then labels us crazy. And what did y'all young folks do? Yup, went ahead and believed them and ignored us when we was out there on the corner begging for somebody to listen. Son, calling someone crazy is the most ignorant thing you can ever say and yo momma knew that. I mean, yeah, she didn't agree with a lot of things I had to say, but at least she listened."

He leaned closer. "Son, I need you to listen to what I'm about to tell you now. Don't just hear me, I need you to *listen*. The truth should be taken in doses, so I'm only going to give you a piece of it, and if you want more - well, you know where to find me."

Cory was engaged. He sat forward with one hand on the table and the other pulling on his chin, clinging to every word that came from the old man's mouth. Cory had never realized how powerful that voice was. His tone was piquing, yet mysterious. The man spoke with a confidence and mannerism that could move mountains.

"Son, what religion are you?" he asked.

Cory was taken back. Although his mother was Catholic, he didn't view himself as a religious person. The times he went to church were when his mother forced him to. Plus, he couldn't even remember the last time he'd cracked open a Bible.

"I'm Catholic, but what does that have to do with anything?" he replied.

"Go get your Bible," the old man ordered.

Cory stared at him with protruding eyes. *What's with this guy?* he thought, rising from his seat and heading to his mother's room. *Mom always kept a Bible on her nightstand; no one had touched anything in that room since she left, so it should still be there.*

To his surprise, the Bible was not there. He searched through all the drawers in the room, but came up empty handed. Cory stood still with a puzzled look on his face.

"Maybe one of them took it," he said to himself, heading downstairs. "Hey, Lana, did you move my mom's Bible?"

"Nope," Lana barked back.

Next, he went to Isabel's room. Isabel was still sick and he regretted waking her, but he had to know.

"Hey, Isabel, did you take Mom's Bible off her night stand?"

"No, but I should have one somewhere in my dresser," Isabel replied.

Cory checked his sister's dresser and found nothing.

"It's not there, Bell."

"Well, it should be," Isabel snapped. "Cory, please. Let me rest."

Cory gave up his search and walked back into the dining room.

"I'll just download it to my cell phone," he said to the old man, who sat back, folded his arms, and nodded.

Pulling out his phone, he searched for Bible apps and then his phone displayed the message, "No Apps Available."

"You won't find it anywhere, son. Have a seat."

Cory sat and put his head down, trying to figure out a logical explanation as to why he couldn't find or get a hold of a Bible.

"Son, I'm gonna be straight with you...yo momma was kidnapped by the Government because she was religious," the old man explained.

"What are you talking about?" Cory interrupted.

"Now, let me say my piece before you interrupt...okay? You must understand that this is bigger than yo momma. It's not just Christianity. It's every religion. The Government are the ones responsible for ATHENS. I'm clueless as to how they did it, but they came up with some sort of a chemical compound that knocked us out for twenty-four hours, and during that time they took away everybody who was religious, including their books and congregations. The meteorites you saw were really just missiles."

"Why?" Lana burst out.

The old man chuckled, "There are three different types of people in this world. One - there're the ones who believe that the state is supreme; two - there're the ones who believe that religion is the supreme ruler, and three, there're the ones that believe that no one can rule them but themselves.

"Now for a very long time, religion was a tool used by conquerors to oppress others. Religion got so big that in some countries, it was put ahead of the state. Every once in a while, in today's society, religion will pop up and challenge the state - resulting in religious wars, terrorist groups, or a whole new regime altogether. Religion is the main threat to state's power. Now, the governments have been looking, just waiting for an opportunity where they can become the supreme ruler again – and it looks like they finally got it."

"But aren't people going to ask questions when they go to a church or mosque or something, and they see that no one's there?" Lana interrupted.

"Darling, the ones that are left still haven't even noticed that their Bibles are missing. The Government took the majority of people that actually cared about their religion, so the few who are left might care for a week or two, then they'll get so caught up in trying to survive that they will forget to follow up on their questions. Over time, religion will fail to exist, and the Government will have no one to answer to," the old man responded.

Cory sat still in his chair, trying to make sense of the startling information being given to him, "Okay, so they get rid of religion, then what?" he asked.

"Then, they will use the basic human necessities to create chaos. Can you imagine how painful it is to die from starvation? Uh-huh, didn't think so. Now imagine that pain to someone who can't die. There's chaos out there, and it's getting worse by the minute.

"The Government is sitting back and letting the people think they rule over themselves while they're the ones who control who eats or drinks. Things will get so bad that the people will literally beg them to intervene. That's when they become the true ruler. But it doesn't stop there. Something big is coming. I'm not sure what - but I will find out."

"So, are you saying there's a cure? And what do you think they've done to my mother?" Cory asked.

"Well, there's got to be a cure," the old man answered. "They had to have something to keep them awake while everybody else was knocked out.

And as for your mom? Son, I have no clue. But if we find her and the rest, we find the answer."

"You seem to know your stuff. Why aren't you missing as well?" Lana questioned.

"Well, I don't believe in God or anything of that nature. You have to understand that religion is more political than it is spiritual. It's all politics! I have spent years studying every religion on the face of the earth, and its ability to give power and take away power cannot be questioned. But that's enough for the day; I'll let this sink in. Thanks for the water." The old man got up and headed toward the door while Cory followed him out.

"Hey, why do you still preach on the corner?"

"I'm recruiting, son, there's a new world order coming, and it's best that we be prepared for it."

"What's your name, and how do you know so much?" Cory asked.

"In due time, son. In due time. Oh, and one more thing, son, whatever you did to that woman, you'd better fix it. He who finds a wife, findeth a good thing."

"She's not my— "

"Til next time, son. Remember, something big is coming. Don't listen to them," the old man said as he walked back to his corner.

Closing the door, Cory stood still and processed everything the old man had said. One thing was certain - he needed to talk to Lana. It was embarrassing that even the old man could sense their tension.

Lana still sat on the couch furthest away from the table. She heard Cory's footsteps and turned her back. Hell hath no fury like a woman scorned.

Cory froze and took a deep breath, bracing himself for another fight, but he hoped that it wouldn't come to that. He sat next to her.

Lana shifted away from him, but it made no difference - unless she got off the couch altogether, and she saw no point in doing that. Besides, as much as she tried to ignore him, she wanted him to apologize for being an asshole.

"Lana, I-, uh I, I…" Cory stuttered.

Lana rolled her eyes and shuffled on the couch. She realized Cory struggled with expressing his emotions, but she was done sympathizing with him. *Can you act like an adult for once and be accountable for your actions?* she thought, her frustration growing by the minute.

"Cory, if you have something to say, then say it. Otherwise, you can move and give me some personal space, okay?" Lana snarled.

Cory was trying to be sincere, but she wasn't making it easy for him. *She's still mad. Clearly, she is not ready to hear me out,* Cory noted. But he had another way to win Lana over.

"We may need to go on another raid. We're running low on some maintenance stuff, and we need to amp up the surveillance. Oh, and medicine for Isabel - it seems like she's getting worse," he said, trying to remain nonchalant and ignore Lana's bad attitude and bitchy expression.

"Okay," she murmured.

Lana tried not to show her excitement. It had been months since their last raid. She wanted more gadgets to play with, of course, but this trip would be different now that the old man seemed to have gotten through to Cory. Perhaps, he would be more open-minded on this raid and search for things other than just supplies. Lana was almost giddy! Now they could try to get to the bottom of what was going on in the world, and what the Government was up to.

"I'll give Doug a call and tell him to expect us tonight," Lana added, trying to maintain her prior disdain.

At last, some peace - even if it had just been for a little while! In that moment in time, she forgot her fury for Cory and her need for his apology. Cory let out a sigh of relief. He hadn't fixed things, but it was a start.

9

Cory and Lana sat in the car, waiting for Doug's text. They had parked behind some bushes near the highway, which was a perfect hiding spot with a clear view of the highway and the exit. They sat in complete silence behind the tinted windows of their unmarked, all-black Audi A5. They used the Audi for raids because of its speed. Otherwise, the car remained in their garage.

Cory wore black jeans and a black sweater with black combat boots that matched his breathable leather gloves, black watch and black baseball cap with the logo ripped off. For protection, he wore a bulletproof vest and a holster underneath that hid both of his guns - a 9mm and a Glock.

Lana wore the same attire, except she had two 9mm pistols tucked under her shirt and a sniper rifle at her feet. Weapons were something they needed. Before the modification to their home, guns they'd gotten from the raids were all they had for protection.

Cory made sure the household knew how to handle a gun. It took several months of training, but after a while, they each became skilled enough to handle their own in any gunfight. Cory wanted Lana and Isabel to avoid close combat, so he had them train with a sniper rifle.

Lana rose to the challenge, and gained impeccable aim and even better precision - and when it came down to it, Cory always felt at ease knowing she was always within safe distance, watching his back.

Lana's phone rested on the dashboard of the car as they waited for Doug to contact them. He was taking longer than usual.

As they waited, Cory and Lana saw the first wave of raiders emerge from hiding when the first trailer truck exited the highway. There was only a driver, with no one in the passenger seat. Lana guessed it was carrying food, and there would be another serviceman in the back, protecting the cargo from raiders.

More often than not, food convoys didn't have many men protecting them – making them easy targets. When the truck stopped at a red light, five cars emerged and followed behind it. Once the light turned green, five more cars emerged, coming in from the front of the truck, creating unexpected traffic for the truck driver as he turned left. Lana followed with her eyes until they drove out of sight.

That was the most organized I've ever seen the raiders, Lana thought. *They surrounded that truck like they were working as a team - but that won't last long. The truck won't last ten minutes down the road before the first car attacks. Then, they will all turn into savages and attack each other. Only two will come back if they even take down the truck. Stupid! Idiots! I hope their brains get put back together for scientists to play with. Exactly what they deserve!*

Lana was still scolding the first set of raiders when the second truck of the night emerged from the highway. Convoys had different destinations. This route saw at least five trucks per night. Some trucks contained food while others had water. Sometimes they were carrying government documents, other times weapons and if they were lucky, medicine or devices and appliances.

The second truck had three people in the front cab, including the driver. Each armed with shotgun rifles. Lana knew right away that the truck was carrying water because of the armory. Water was more precious than food due to the contamination and the Government refusing to maintain the plumbing systems.

I really hope Doug is smart enough to get us some water since Cory thinks it's okay to invite guests to drink what we risk our lives getting.

Lana knew there were at least two more men in the back of the truck protecting the precious water. This made attacking the cargo all but impossible. Even if the raiders slowed down or even stopped the truck, once the armed men in the truck felt threatened, they attacked.

As the second truck pulled up to the red light, two raggedy cars drove up beside it. They must have realized something valuable was inside because they didn't wait for the light like before. Three men hopped out carrying weapons, big pliers, and a homemade torch. To Lana's surprise, the truck didn't move - although it was an ambush.

The raider holding the torch turned it on and set it to work on the back doors of the truck, while the other two kept watch on the driver's and passenger's doors to see if the servicemen would get out. None of them thought to look up.

They should have.

A serviceman on the roof shot twice at the raider with the torch. His fingers flew off his hand like little pieces of crumbs falling off crackers. The man wailed and dropped the torch and ran back to the car. He didn't make it far. The serviceman finished the job with a shot to the head.

At the first sign of trouble, the two rusted cars fled, leaving the remaining raiders defenseless. They had no choice but to attack the serviceman on top.

The serviceman shielded off their attacks until the raiders exhausted their firepower. It was only a matter of time now. With their attention focused on the roof, the two servicemen from the front blind-sided the raiders. A few shots knocked them to the ground. They didn't shoot to kill, but soon the raiders wished they had.

Drawing out batons, they beat the wounded raiders, not to just subdue them; they wanted to send a message. In an act of sheer inhumanity, they stood and cackled as they set the raiders on fire. Hysterical screams could be heard for miles as the wind carried the stench of burnt skin.

Not once did Lana flinch; the world had made her numb to things like this. She sat and watched the two men crawl around as the flames grew into bigger blaze. At first, she could make out the men in the fire, but soon, the men disappeared— and so did their screams.

The truck drove off, leaving the two raiders on the ground burnt to a crisp. The war zone between servicemen and the raiders continued all night. As convoys passed, raiders attacked them either at the highway exit, or followed them further onto the main road. Many cars would follow the convoys, but only one or two would come back, full of food and water.

Inevitably, raiders began to attack each other, realizing it was easier than attacking a large trailer truck with trained servicemen. That was what worried Lana the most—getting attacked on their way back home. But so far, they had avoided that by taking less traveled roads, or by waiting until most raiders had already gone home themselves.

10

Cory was beginning to worry.

"Hey, where is this guy? He's an hour late. I don't want any trouble... we're leaving," he declared.

They had left Isabel alone, and her fever was getting worse. Along with the growing feeling something had gone wrong, he didn't want to be waiting on some guy when he could be home taking care of his sister.

"No," Lana barked.

Cory's skin prickled, her attitude reinforced his suspicion.

"What did you do?" he asked.

"Nothing. It's just that...I've been waiting for months to add new cameras outside...I'm not leaving them," Lana lied as she looked away.

Doug was taking longer than usual because she had asked him to stop a special truck. It should contain detailed military and government documents, a clue of whatever the government was doing. It might provide the motivation Cory needed to restart his search for his mother.

"I'm not buying that for one second, and I'll ask you this once more - what did you do?" Cory said, all the more suspicious for the lack of eye contact from Lana.

"Look, I didn't do anything, okay? I just told him we wanted to do a raid. Maybe he got caught up with the other raiders..."

The vibration from her phone interrupted Lana's rant. *Perfect timing,* she thought. She grabbed her phone and read Cory the rendezvous point.

Doug had brought three trailer trucks into a big airplane hangar located almost two hours away from where Cory and Lana lived. They didn't mind - the farther it was, the better for them, and the stronger the guarantee of fewer people knowing what they were doing. As soon as they arrived, Doug greeted them, along with six armed raiders.

Doug was a tall, skinny, Irishman with ginger hair and eyes as blue as the ocean. He was handsome, and his infatuation for Lana made Cory uneasy.

"Sup, Lana?" Doug smiled, leaning against the truck. "Wasn't expecting to hear from you anytime soon."

Lana couldn't help but smile back. Although his perverted interest was annoying, he was quite charming, and despite Cory's presence, Lana still went along with him. It was her way of getting back at Cory for acting like a jerk.

"We want some new stuff," Lana winked.

Cory grunted and glared at Doug. "Can we hurry this up?" he said. "Let's get what we came here for and go," he whispered to Lana before walking to the first truck.

"We don't need food, we have lots of that. We need water. I think two five-liter bottles will do," Lana informed Doug as they climbed into the first truck, joining Cory.

"Yeah, there's water in the back there. I even got some vitamin water – all types of flavors. I saved those for you," Doug smiled.

Cory shook his head, trying to get rid of the bad taste in his mouth. He hated the man, but he had to control his temper. Doug was an asset – a valuable one at that.

The second truck had weapons as well as cameras and other devices to update Lana's systems and maintain their fortress of a home. Cory wasn't too keen on the details of how Lana maintained everything - he surveyed the truck once and then sat at the door waiting for Lana to take what she needed.

"Hey, Cory," Lana drawled, "why don't you check the last truck with Doug. I have a few things to collect here, and you're not doing anything. When I have what I need, I'll come over to you guys."

Cory wasn't thrilled with her suggested, but complied, mostly because Doug would be with him. Doug ordered two of the raiders to watch Lana while he took Cory over to the last truck.

"Well, I hope you'll find something interesting in here. Lana was specific about what she wanted…she's smart, and for some reason, she thinks you are too. I don't see it, but hey, what do I know," Doug jeered as they hopped inside.

Smart-ass! - Another reason Cory hated him! A quick glance at the two armed men standing behind them made Cory think twice about making Doug eat his words. Regardless, he would not let some low-life commando wanna-be insult his intelligence. Puffing up his chest, he turned to face Doug, as the pair of armed men inched closer.

They stood there, glaring at each other, refusing to show any sign of weakness. They were the same height, but Cory's physique was more imposing, and he wanted Doug to know it, and in front of his gang. He wanted to remind Doug he was superior to him in every way. He stood there and watched as Doug's grin faded bit by bit, before chuckling to himself.

"Just like I thought - now move along, so I can see what's inside," Cory snarled.

Feeling disrespected, Doug grunted loudly as he crossed his arms, challenging Cory to act.

Great! Another tough guy, Cory thought as he assessed the situation. He wanted nothing more than to pummel Doug's face until it turned blue. But the MGP-84 machine pistols Doug's men had pointed at his head, ready to fire if he even flinched at Doug the wrong way caused him to show restraint. Cory chuckled and brushed past him as he walked toward the wooden crates, stacked from the floor to the ceiling.

Cory spotted a smaller crate toward the back that appeared out of place. It had unusual markings on the side that heightened his suspicions. The top of the box read in big, bold red letters: **To Damian Phillips**, **CONFIDENTIAL** and **HANDLE WITH CARE**.

Well, this looks promising, Cory thought.

"Pass me the crowbar," he barked at one of the armed thugs.

He'd hoped this crate would give him an idea of what was in the other boxes, avoiding having to go through them one by one. Prying off the top, the box did nothing, but instill more confusion. Inside the crate, were blueprints, neatly rolled and placed one on top of another in an organized fashion.

"What is all of this?" Cory said, unrolling the first blueprint from the box.

He couldn't help feeling he had stumbled on something important. At first glance, they appeared to be floor plans for a building, but it seemed far too complicated to be a mere sketch of a construction site. They were more like the blueprints Lana would make when she created new devices. Decrypting the formulas printed in white ink would be difficult, if not impossible. Frustrated, Cory rolled the blueprint back up. No point looking at it further, it would take Lana to figure out what the drawings represented.

Looking for more general clues, he opened some of the bigger crates. Inside were small black rectangular devices, each in a clear protective plastic. They looked like USB flash drives that plugged into computers. Cory took a device and held it up to get a better view.

After removing the plastics, he massaged it. Sliding his fingers across one side of the device while twirling it between his fingers, he was startled as it popped open to reveal a tiny computer chip. The chip was very thin and rectangular and looked like the SIM cards found in cell phones. It had two slender, smooth flat surfaces - one white and the other black. The white side had tiny green wires in patterns.

"What is this?" Cory asked once more, hoping his question wouldn't go unanswered.

"Not sure what it is. They're sending out about a hundred and fifty trucks just like this - with the same stuff inside - to every major city across the country. Rumor has it that they're distributing these things all over the world. I thought this would be something Lana would be interested in," Doug informed.

"All right, " Cory sneered, still showing his animosity.

After opening five more boxes, he realized they all had the same small devices inside. *This is crazy,* Cory thought for the hundredth time. It didn't take rocket science to recognize that he had stumbled upon something important, and he wanted to figure out what these mysterious chips were, and why they were being delivered to every city in the world.

When Lana entered the truck, Cory was sitting on the floor rubbing the tiny computer chip in the palm of his hand.

"Whoa! What's that?" she said, intrigued.

"Beats me…some sort of computer chip," Cory replied as he stood up and turned to the others. "We're taking whatever Lana has and these two boxes," he ordered, pointing at the smaller crates with the blueprints and one with the computer chips. "Doug, you know anything at all about what these are and what they do?"

He looked straight at Doug to determine the level of honesty in his response.

"Nope, I just have their delivery information. They began distribution about two days ago. They're pretty well guarded - more so even than water. Oh, and they go to every city - about the same number as the registered population. That's all I got," Doug responded, shrugging his shoulder before turning his full attention to Lana. "So, for all the stuff you guys are taking, and the risk I took to get them here...how will my services be paid for?"

"How much do you want?" Cory answered.

He scanned Cory up and down with confidence before he said, "$2,000 for the crates, $3,000 for my resources."

Five thousand dollars was a lot of money, especially now the majority of the population was living on only pennies a day. Lana had almost that much left over from what her grandmother had sent, and Cory had $1,500 saved up from previous raids. But no way was he going to give Doug as much as he wanted.

"I don't have $5,000, Doug."

"Well, what do you have?"

"I have $1,000," Cory lied.

"Well, that will get you two crates of water, but everything else stays here, and it'll go to the highest bidder," Doug smirked.

Especially with the attitude Cory gave him, Doug enjoyed the ultimate leverage he had when it came down to negotiating for the merchandise he had just stolen.

"Come on, man, how about if I give you the $1,000 and then you wait till we sell the other stuff, and I'll give you 80% off that?" Cory pleaded.

Doug thought about the offer. Of course, he would accept it, but he was having fun toying with Cory's sudden interest in the merchandise.

"Okay, I'll take it. But only if Lana upgrades the security system in my new house," he said with one eyebrow raised.

As much as Cory hated the thought of Lana going to Doug's house, it was more than reasonable for what they were getting in return. They shook hands in agreement and Lana and Cory headed back to their car. Doug ordered his armed raiders to carry their crates to the Audi.

"I look forward to hearing from y'all real soon," Doug smiled as he watched them climb back into their vehicle.

"Cory, let's do his security as soon as possible. Doug isn't someone who should be played with," Lana cautioned.

"Yeah, tell me about it. I'll hit him up tomorrow."

Cory drove silently as they began their long trip home, giving Lana plenty of time to reminisce how organized the raids had become. Most of the risk had been reduced, and the quality of merchandise had increased.

***

It certainly didn't start that way. In the beginning, going on raids was stressful and filled with life-threatening situations. Most times the items they got didn't justify the risk. Cory started raiding alone and had no clue how to go about it. Others were overtaking convoys as they drove from city to city, but many people got hurt on those raids too. Not only were there armed servicemen, he also had to factor in the other raiders who weren't going to share the items in the trucks.

To participate in raids, you needed information about what each truck contained, the roads the convoys traveled, and what times they would go through certain cities. It was all but impossible to get that kind of information.

Cory proved resourceful by getting David, a friend from the days of playing basketball, to share his information. David was one of the few people Cory still talked to after The Sabbath.

David got his information from his older brother, Mike, who had just gotten a job as a serviceman. When he heard Cory wanted in on the raid, he was willing to do more than help them.

He met up with Cory and talked him through how the raids operated. Concerned for his safety, he explained how dangerous it was and how the majority of people who went on a raid got hurt, and over half of those people ended up on the brink of death.

Mike took a liking to Cory - so much so, that he provided Cory with intel on future raids at no charge, as long as he was careful and trusted none of the other raiders.

Cory, knowing the danger, made sure Lana and Isabel knew the proper use of firearms - not just for raids, but for their safety at home as well. He figured it would relieve some of the anxieties he felt when he had to leave the girls at home alone.

Lana smiled as she remembered getting ready for her first raid. Isabel had refused to go. She was uncomfortable with fighting, and she couldn't stomach the grotesque things she might see. The first raid Lana went on was with Cory and David. That night, David and two of his friends, Jamal and Jeremiah, drove a black SUV van to Cory's house. Lana heard them coming. They had the Wu-Tang blaring through their speakers, shaking every single house they passed. They parked in the driveway and waited for Cory to come outside while Lana was inside begging Cory not to go.

"Come on, Cory," she begged. "David is an idiot, and he's reckless. He's always been this way, getting into fights, abusing girls and drugs. What if something happens to you?"

"Cory," Isabel added, "this guy is bad news. I don't want you to go tonight, please."

"Look, you're both being ridiculous. Have you noticed how we're living right now? We need water and food. If I have to eat ramen noodles one more time, I will die - literally just curl up and die," Cory yelled at the both of them out of frustration.

"Well, why can't we go by ourselves? Mike already told you what to do," Lana reasoned. "We can do it ourselves."

Cory took a deep breath as he shook his head.

"Lana, I'm going with them," Cory affirmed. "If you want to come, grab your vest and your gun. If you continue to complain with Isabel, then stay home. I don't need any more stress."

Cory marched toward the door, and without saying another word, Lana followed. She turned to Isabel and mouthed, "Bye." As the door shut, she saw tears streaming down Isabel's face. She was heartbroken, but she wouldn't be able to forgive herself if anything happened to Cory and she wasn't there. Walking to David's van, Lana said silent prayers, one for her and Cory, and one for Isabel.

"What's up guys?" Cory said as they hopped in the car.

"About time," Jamal replied as he sped down the street. "We're on a tight schedule."

Lana settled in next to Cory. She put her head down as she texted Isabel, and out of the corner of her eye she noticed Jeremiah peeking down her shirt. *Pervert,* she thought, crossing her arms, blocking his view. She had never met him before. If she weren't so disgusted, she would have even considered him handsome. His cheekbones made him pretty and dangerous, but it was his lips and his smile that were the real charmers. His smile was a spell that could put a girl into a trance.

While Jeremiah was watching Lana, Jamal explained their game plan.

"Okay, listen up, because I'll say this once. We're hitting up two trucks. One has food and the other has water. The one with food will be easy. But the one with water will be challenging. David's brother is guarding the food truck and he agreed to hook us up — so let's pray the other raiders haven't gotten to him first. The second truck will be old school."

"Old school is my type of party," Jeremiah cackled.

"Focus," Jamal scolded. "Now, we will attack from the front. The trucks are hard to run over, so we will park in the middle of the road and force the driver to stop or at least slow down. When he does, Jeremiah and David will exit the van and pretend that we have a flat tire. We have tools underneath that we will use to burn the engine of the truck. This way they can't drive off.

"Now, the second truck has two servicemen guarding the water in back. The serviceman with the driver will be David's job. David, make sure you bust his ass before he can do anything. Jeremiah, you will take care of the servicemen in the back."

"So what do we do?" Lana asked Jamal.

"Follow Jeremiah. If he needs backup, the two of you will help. It's simple. Don't get fucked up - you do the fucking up. Got that, Princess?"

"Yes, I got it. Take their stuff, and don't get hurt. Not rocket science," she boasted, trying to mask her anxiety.

David, along with his friends, had dark chocolate skin with well-defined facial features, making them look more like fashion models than petty thugs. Each had a broad muscular physique - as Lana thought more about it, it made sense. David was on the football team at school; where he likely met Jamal and Jeremiah. But despite their looks, Jamal was by far the scariest in the crew. There was something about him that struck fear into her heart.

Jeremiah interrupted her thoughts. "Did you guys bring weapons?"

"Yeah, we're prepared," Cory responded.

"Do you know how to use them?" he asked.

"Yes, we're good," Cory added. He had watched Jeremiah staring at Lana and didn't like him.

They were zooming down a one-lane highway in the middle of nowhere. It was dark except for the faint light of the few scattered lampposts revealing only trees and bushes for miles. The car had slowed down to twenty-five miles per hour instead of the ninety it had been doing.

"Okay, get ready - here comes the truck," Jamal barked. "Oh, and Princess, be careful, you're too pretty for all this."

With Jeremiah staring at her as if he wanted to pounce on her and Jamal's blatant teasing, Lana's fear had turned to aggravation. As the van came to a screeching halt, the truck pulled up behind them.

Full of adrenaline, Lana's heart was beating rapidly. The time had come. David and Jeremiah jumped out of the van. They gave each other a nod and walked toward the back right tire.

David stooped down and reached under the van; meanwhile, the passenger door of the truck opened and a serviceman hopped out.

"Hey, get the fuck off the road," he hollered, waving his gun in the air.

David jolted up and swung as if he was throwing a baseball, something shiny flew and landed between the serviceman's eyes. Another followed and landed in the center of his forehead. Lana gasped as the serviceman stood in the middle of the road, eyes wide and bulging.

Blood ran down the middle of his face. He made a soft grunt and fell to the ground. Before she could process what had just happened, Jeremiah was at the hood of the truck. He stuck a device onto the hood and within seconds, smoke poured out of the truck's engine. The truck made a popping sound, and then BANG. Lana jumped from the thunderous sound, but Jeremiah didn't flinch. He moved to the driver's side of the truck, and placed a second device near the door handle. Within seconds, he had the door open, and dragged the driver out. He called to Cory.

"Shoot him," he ordered.

"What? No. Don't do it, Cory," Lana yelled. "This isn't us."

"Quiet, Lana!" Cory replied, then turned his attention back to Jeremiah, "Why do I have to shoot him? Look at him, he's no threat to us."

"It's a lesson you have to learn. You can't spare anyone on these raids. You think he's not armed; he's waiting for the perfect time to grab his knife strapped to his ankle. He will cut your throat and watch you bleed out. Do you know what it's like to bleed out but not die?" Jeremiah asked.

Cory shook his head.

"Well, you will if you don't shoot him," Jeremiah added.

Cory worried on what would happen if he didn't follow through. He wouldn't risk putting Lana's life in jeopardy. Grabbing his gun, he aimed it at the driver's head. But he couldn't pull the trigger. This man had done nothing to him.

The driver looked at him, his eyes narrowed.

"He's right. If you let me go, I'll gut all of you like fish and then fuck her while you all bleed out…"

Jeremiah pulled the trigger before the driver could finish his sentence. His brains splattered on the side of the truck.

Monsters - was the only word that came to Lana's mind when she thought about Cory's filthy friends.

***

The memory was still as vivid and shocking as it had been during her first raid. She wondered once more what happened to the driver, and if he had recovered from that shot to his head. Shaking it off, she breathed in deeply and turned toward Cory, wanting to talk to break out of her painful recollections. His face was set and eyes straight ahead. He was still wrapped in his own thoughts as he continued to drive in total silence.

There was little hope of a meaningful conversation with him when he was closed off like this. She resumed staring out the window into the darkness. Before long, memories of that first raid flooded in again.

***

"I saw your face - you were about to pull that trigger when he mentioned what he would do to her! Well, at least now I know how to get a reaction out of you - all I have to do is threaten the Princess," Jeremiah joked as they walked to the back of the truck.

Reaching for the latch, Jamal said, "David's bro should be inside, but in case he's not, be prepared to attack."

The back door of the truck opened and Mike jumped down.

"Ahh, my brothers," Mike greeted, "What's up?"

Jeremiah smiled, "Just out here hustling, getting the bread to feed the fam."

Lana and Cory opened the truck door wider and peered inside. There was so much food. It was a mobile grocery store, except they didn't have to pay. Lana wanted to jump for joy, but she controlled herself, remembering whom she was with. When they had taken all they wanted, Mike instructed them what to do next.

"I already called in and told them I've been hit. Reinforcement should be here in ten. I'll be fine. You guys go on now, and be careful," Mike said.

As they all settled inside the van, David hopped back out and walked up to Mike, "Hey, you forgot something."

He punched Mike in the face. Mike stumbled backwards then smiled.

"You're always so eager to do that," Mike said as he spat out blood.

"Got to make it believable, don't want you to get fired or anything," David said as he hopped back into the van.

"All right kids, the same thing this time, except everyone gets fucked up in this truck. And change of plans, the princess gets a special job. She'll deal with the guard in the back first," Jamal ordered.

Lana swallowed. She was prepared to do what she had to, but if they were expecting her to turn into a savage, they would be disappointed. She wasn't going to sacrifice her humanity for the entertainment of a few sickos. But her knight in shining armor saw her distress and spoke out.

"She isn't doing it," Cory said.

The van stopped and everyone went quiet. David looked at Cory's face, then glanced down at his hands. Cory was gripping his gun, with his index finger twitching. He recognized Cory wasn't playing games, and neither was his friend. He had to diffuse the situation before it escalated.

"Okay, okay, I'll let Lana lead. But I take the guy out. Cool?" he said.

"Yeah, whatever," Cory replied.

David let out the breath he had been holding and nodded.

They did everything the same with the next truck they stopped, except this time Cory knocked out the servicemen and Jeremiah handled the driver. Walking to the back, they let Lana lead.

She was trembling with fear and adrenaline. Her gun was in her hand, but all she wanted to do was hide behind the four men with her.

Jamal broke the lock then eased the back door open. There were two servicemen, but just one was armed and ready in the back. Without hesitation, Lana shot the serviceman in the arm, causing him to drop his gun. He cried out in pain as Jeremiah laughed.

"That won't do anything," Jeremiah said.

Before he could tell Lana to shoot the man in the head, David shot the serviceman in the stomach and then in the chest.

"I don't want brains all over the water. I want to be able to drink it," David shrugged.

The second serviceman was sitting with both hands up in the air and his gun by his feet.

"Well, do the next one now," Jamal ordered Lana.

"No," Lana boomed. "He's not armed. He threw his gun away."

"You're right, Princess, but he still gets it," Jeremiah added.

Cory couldn't take the blatant disrespect any longer. He raised his gun, aiming it at Jeremiah's head.

"Lana, watch my back," he ordered. "Now, I told you motherfuckers, she ain't doing shit!"

Guns pointed in every direction while Jeremiah had his hands up, begging the others not to shoot. Things were getting ugly, and might have exploded if it wasn't for the serviceman.

"Wait, don't shoot," the serviceman implored. He tried to stand, but his knees buckled.

Everyone turned to gawk at the serviceman who would have been caught in the crossfire.

"Look, my name is Doug… I-I have a proposition," he stuttered.

"What about it?" David demanded, now pointing his gun at Doug.

Doug took a loud gulp.

"Look, you guys are risking your lives for plain food and water. I can hook you up with the exotic foods, fancy water, and a whole bunch of stuff that the Government has kept from you. You're doing small time stuff; I'm here working on the big-time. I have inside connections, where you'll never have to fight with anybody again. Let me be your inside man. If I don't deliver, then you can do whatever you want with me."

Doug finished his speech and no one said or did anything.

"Listen, if you don't believe me then let me get the crate and show you what I have inside," Doug coaxed.

"Okay, but let me pat you down first," Jamal said.

"Fair enough," Doug replied.

That was the first time they had met Doug, and Cory knew how he would capitalize on this. He needed an inside man of his own, and he wasn't comfortable with how David and his friends handled things. Blowing people's brains out was never his style.

At first, they didn't trust Doug, but he delivered every time and eventually, Mike had been promoted and moved the crew away, leaving Cory and Lana to work with Doug alone. Lana thought they needed to build a better business relationship where Doug had mutual respect for them and wasn't doing things out of fear. She decided to give some of the money from her grandmother to Doug as a token of their appreciation.

***

Blinking away the memories, Lana realized Doug aided them in a big way. He made it possible for them to have so much more than anyone she knew - in particular, the people living in their neighborhood. Because of Doug, they could live a decent life and now perhaps find Cory's mother.

Cracking a smile, she was content with the events of this evening. She dozed off thinking about what kind of information the devices they'd found might have and all the insight it could give them.

She woke as Cory parked the car at the house.

"C'mon, Lana. This stuff needs to get unloaded before it gets light."

"You did good with Doug tonight," she said. His head whipped around, his eyes drilling into hers. She flinched and said, "I mean with the deal you made." Lana sighed and rubbed her eyes.

"Thanks babe. I thought you'd like going over to his new house. But don't think for a minute I'm going to leave him with you alone. I don't trust him."

Or me either, Lana thought. It seems these days the only time he paid attention to her was when he needed to protect her, or was working up a fit of jealousy. Lana exhaled loudly, picked up the small crate and followed Cory inside.

"And, Cory, don't call me 'babe,' you haven't earned that back yet."

11

Cory woke up the next morning to the sounds of Isabel preparing bath water in the kitchen.

"Morning, Bell. How are you feeling today?" he asked, stretching his arms.

Isabel looked into the living room and chuckled at the sight of her brother on the couch.

"Much better, thanks - but why are you sleeping on the couch?" she asked.

"Lana's tripping again," Cory responded.

"You've got to treat that girl better, Cory— "

"Not now," Cory interrupted as he got up and walked toward the kitchen.

"Uh-huh, you better listen before she leaves you, then you'll be the one crying," Isabel teased.

"Yeah, so I'm guessing you slept through all the commotion then, huh."

"Why, what happened?" Isabel asked sounding more intrigued.

"Oh, nothing," Cory said, changing the subject, "but you remember that old man that's always on our street? Yeah, well, he was here the other day."

"Huh? Why?"

"Just to talk. Some of the things he said made a lot of sense. He even said that the Government took mom."

Wrinkles of surprise appeared on her forehead. It was the first time Cory had mentioned their mother in a conversation that wasn't an argument.

"Well, do you believe him?" Isabel asked.

"Not sure, but I'll find out. I got something from the raid last night. Lana's looking at it; hopefully it'll give us some answers."

"We've got to bring her home, Cory," Isabel said as she carried her bath water to the bathroom. Smiling, she was happy her younger brother was finally taking initiative to look for their missing mother.

Cory had arranged a meeting with Doug for six p.m. That gave them plenty of time to investigate the contents of the crates. It was already ten, and Cory wanted Lana to analyze the devices and blueprints as soon as possible.

Walking toward his room, he grabbed the doorknob and to his surprise, it wasn't locked. No one was inside. He headed to the basement where Lana liked to work. He was pleased she had already examined the device. When Cory walked in, Lana's face was stuck to her microscope, and she didn't even bother to acknowledge his presence.

"Hey, you're up early. What time did you get up?" Cory asked.

"Four hours ago," she replied, without moving her head.

"Any news on what we're looking at?"

Lana rolled her chair back to the computer behind her, and pulled her research up onto the screen.

"Well, one thing's for sure - the blueprint you got yesterday is for that device. It's not giving me much, though. My guess is that the blueprint highlights a certain function that the chip does. What that function is…well, I still need more research, but the chip itself is amazing.

"It appears to be biometric, by the looks of it, and check out this silicon hidden inside the chip! It's a picture of the sun, and inside the sun, there's a picture of a human's brain. Maybe they're trying to control us. You think they're trying to control us?" Lana was speaking too fast, and before Cory could answer her, she changed the subject.

"Well, I took the image of the silicon and compared it to the blueprints you gave me and check this out! It's the same. Well, not the picture of the sun, but the brain inside the sun, the blueprint is in the shape of a human brain."

"Okay, hold up. What do you mean by 'it's biometric?' And what's all this talk about control? And why is there a picture inside a freaking computer chip?" Cory asked.

Lana palmed her forehead, realizing she was speaking in a foreign language to Cory.

"Sorry. Well, biometric means a sophisticated device that can identify you. But instead of using ID cards, it can use your physical characteristics - like your face, fingerprints, irises, or veins, or even behavioral characteristics like your voice, or handwriting to know who you are.

"I'm willing to bet this chip will control our behavior or something along those lines. And they usually create images inside computer chips for authenticity. Something to tell the difference between the real and the fake. But I need more time and more information. I'm not going to get much more from this blueprint and device."

"Okay. Maybe I'll mention this to the old man and see if he knows anything. But I'll leave you to your work. We have to head to Doug's in a few, so don't overdo it."

"All right, be up there in a bit," Lana said as Cory climbed the stairs.

Poking his head out the living room window, Cory saw the old man was preaching on the street corner. He thought about inviting him over to talk again, but figured he'd wait until Lana finished her research. However, he hadn't thought it would take her five hours to do so.

*

Cory was in his room when Lana walked in and judging by her facial expression, he could tell she was drained.

"How did it go?" he asked.

"Ugh, I can't figure it out. I tried running a diagnostic, but there's an encryption on it that's like impossible to crack," she replied.

"Don't worry, we'll get more info."

"Yeah...how's Isabel?"

"She's doing much better; she 's in her room right now."

"Well, let me get something to eat, then we can head over to Doug's," Lana said as she walked out and headed into the kitchen.

She fixed herself a bowl of noodles, and as soon as she was done, she grabbed her bag of equipment while Cory snatched the keys to his mother's old silver Nissan from the kitchen counter.

It was a warm afternoon. Music blared from knots of people on the corners. Occasionally, a scream for help was heard, but no one seemed to care - including Cory and Lana. The only way to live in peace was not to meddle in the affairs of others.

Trash and dirty, used needles littered the sidewalk. Prostitutes streamed in and out of abandoned buildings and shadows struck fear in anyone who walked near them. Ragged children with swollen bellies were running and playing, looking like they hadn't bathed in ages. People wandered outside their homes doing anything and everything to escape reality. A stench of rotten flesh, dead rodents, alcohol, and cheap sex hovered over their neighborhood.

Strangers stood out like nuns at a bar. After The Sabbath, the people in Cory's neighborhood made it their business to get to know those living around them. Anyone new entering their neighborhood got noticed at once - especially females. The folks who belonged there earned the right to roam without harassment from others.

Cory glared at anyone who dared to meet his gaze. Ever since Lana had been attacked, word spread that Cory wasn't one to be tampered with. They climbed into his mother's car and drove to Doug's house. He lived just twenty minutes away in a cottage in the middle of the woods; completely isolated from the dangers of the city life. The worst thing he had to worry about would be a bear knocking on his front door. Doug was already outside doing yard work when they pulled up to his house.

"Ah! Welcome to my humble abode!" Doug hollered with his arms opened wide.

"Wow, this is your new place? I'm jealous, Doug," Lana responded, embracing the scenic view.

"Well, you don't have to be…you're more than welcome to stay," Doug flirted. Cory laughed it off.

Inside, Cory felt like a ghost floating around in the background - just what Doug wanted. After a quick tour, they gathered in the living room. Lana was still in awe of Doug's home, filled with state of the art furniture and appliances, but Cory was not nearly as impressed.

"Looks like being a corrupt government official really does pay off," Cory said.

Lana gawked at Cory, disgust in her eyes.

"Mind your tongue boy! Your life would be shit if not for me," Doug fired back.

Doug made a valid point; they were a lot more fortunate than most people he came in contact with, and a great deal of that was because of Doug.

"Sorry, Doug," Lana said, trying to soothe him. "I have no idea what's gotten into him."

They continued to talk, leaving Cory quiet in the background. After thirty minutes had gone by, Cory wondered when Lana would get to work on the security system. Grabbing his phone, he messaged Isabel to make sure everything was all right at home and gave them another ten minutes. Time flew by as Cory sat and watched Lana and Doug talk about everything except the security system.

"Yo! Can we please get to work?" Cory interrupted, reminding them why they were there.

Lana had been so caught up in the conversation, she had forgotten the purpose of their visit, and even forgot Cory was sitting right beside her. Cory looked irritated, but he had waited long enough before his outburst, so, instead of lashing back, she concurred with Cory's request.

"Well, I don't have a security system installed right now; just have the equipment in the basement laid out for you. I was wondering if you could set up the cameras today, and then we'll go from there," Doug said as he led them down. "How long will it take?"

"Well, first I need the blueprints of the house, then you need to show me where you want the cameras installed. Depending on how many cameras and what kind of system you want, I need a couple of hours at least," Lana replied.

Cory sighed at the idea of being in Doug's house that long. His annoyance caught Doug's attention.

"Hey," he drawled. "you can leave and come back to get her later if you like."

Cory thought about leaving Doug alone with Lana.

"Nope," he answered, "I'm good."

They sat and watched Lana toying with the equipment. Cory's phone rang. It was Isabel calling.

"Bell, what's up?"

"Cory," Isabel whispered, "there's strange guys outside the house."

Cory's body stiffened, "What do you mean by strange guys? What do they look like? What are they doing?"

"There's about six of them roaming the streets, they're all wearing black uniforms and have guns...they look like they're searching for something," Isabel said with a trembling voice.

"Isabel, have they come to the door?"

"Yes, they knocked. But I stayed quiet, and they moved on to other houses."

"You did good, Isabel. I want you to go down into the cellar and stay put, I'm on my way right now."

"Cory," Isabel said with her voice cracking, "please hurry, I'm scared. They started picking people off the streets and everyone ran inside."

"Keep your phone on you. I'm on my way right now!"

Cory hung up, and Lana was right in his face.

"What's going on, Cory?" she asked.

"I don't know, but I have to go back home to check on things."

"I'm coming with you," Lana said.

"No, no, stay here," Cory said, not wanting to put Lana in harm's way. "I'm sure it's nothing, keep your cell on you, I'll call."

Judging by the look on Cory's face, Lana knew that no matter what, she would not change his mind.

"Okay, but call me right away," she said as she watched Cory rush upstairs.

12

Lana shook off negative thoughts. She knew the safest place Isabel could be was inside their home.

"I'm sure everything is all right," Doug said, trying to comfort her.

"Yeah, you're probably right...now, how about that security system."

Lana was glad she at least had something to do to keep her mind off things. Plus, she enjoyed Doug's company. They stayed in the basement for a while. Lana was getting the cameras ready while talking to Doug about their lives before The Sabbath.

Lana had imagined that Doug would become sexual toward her, but to her surprise, he seemed very sensitive to the situation and acted like a complete gentleman. The more Doug talked about his past relationships, the more she realized how funny he was.

Lana couldn't stop laughing. *Wow, I haven't laughed like this since the times Cory used to tell me about his girls...shit! Cory!*

Lana grabbed her phone.

"Hey, everything OK?" she messaged.

Cory responded within a couple of minutes.

"All good. Nobody is on the streets. Bell's still scared, waiting til she's calm before coming to get you," he texted back.

Lana was relieved that Isabel was safe, but furious with Cory. *He didn't even have the decency to call me and tell me that everything's all right. I had to message him...he doesn't care about me — not if I'm safe, or if I'm worried to death.*

"Lana, is everything all right?" Doug asked, interrupting her thoughts.

"Yes, everything's fine. Cory just messaged me," Lana said, trying her hardest to conceal her true frustration. "Now, why don't we go outside and install these things?"

Lana grabbed a few cameras and the blueprints and followed Doug outside. Doug grabbed a toolbox and ladder from the shed, and they began installing the security cameras.

"I'm so useless," Doug said, looking up at Lana.

"Huh, what?" Lana said, not sure of what he meant.

"I mean, you're up there with the power drill, and look at me…I'm down here holding on to the ladder for you."

Lana laughed.

"Stop it! Every woman needs a strong man to hold her up," she winked.

"Hey, how'd you get so smart, anyway? I bet you fix everything in the house while he does nothing but sits there, right?"

Lana laughed again, "Let's just say I had few friends growing up, so books kept me company. In school, all the girls wanted to do was mock me, and all the guys wanted was for me to do their homework or to have sex. The only things I trusted were my books, so our relationship grew, and so did my brain."

"So which one does Cory want? Homework or sex?" Doug joked.

"I don't know if he wants anything from me anymore," Lana sulked.

They mounted one more camera on the edge of the house in silence as it began to get dark. Doug called it quits and led Lana back inside.

"We'll schedule another date to finish setting up the cameras and the wiring," Lana promised as Doug left her sitting on the couch as he walked toward the kitchen.

"Want some water?" he called out.

"Yes, thank you, that's mighty generous of you," she replied.

Doug returned with a glass of water in one hand and a beige folder in the other. He handed Lana the water and made himself comfortable next to her.

"Thanks for coming and helping out with my new pad."

Lana was flattered; it has been a while since someone had made her feel appreciated, "Aw, Doug you don't have to thank me, plus you're always looking out for me."

"Well, I got this for you," Doug said as he handed her the beige folder.

"What's this?" Lana asked.

"Some government documents I picked up. I can't read it, so I figured it might benefit you…I can tell that Cory lost someone important to him, that's probably why he's so protective of you, but you don't owe him anything. Before you open that folder, I want you to think long and hard about what you're getting yourself into. Shit, he's not the only one who cares for you."

Lana looked at the folder once more. It was a thick folder about two inches in width, and on the front it read, **Damian Phils.**

"Thank you," she smiled, "for everything."

Lana got up and went to the basement to get her things. She put the folder in her bag, making sure she left nothing behind before heading back upstairs. This was a new side of Doug, and it was refreshing. As soon as Lana returned to Doug, her phone vibrated.

"It's Cory, he said he's leaving home in five minutes, and he'll be here in thirty," Lana said out loud.

Lana realized with a jolt she was annoyed that Cory was on his way. She'd enjoyed her time with Doug. He reminded her of how Cory used to be before The Sabbath. Lost in her thoughts, she caught herself staring at Doug.

They were only inches apart, looking into each other eyes. Doug leaned over and kissed Lana on the lips, then pulled back.

Lana froze, not sure of what to do. In the past, she would have slapped him for even trying to touch her, but instead, Lana leaned her face forward, grabbing the back of his head and kissed him back. Before long, Doug was on top of her, kissing and touching her body. It seemed so natural at first, but then she came to her senses.

Doug, Doug, Doug…Cory!

Snapping out of her pleasure, she began pleading with Doug to stop. Doug lowered his hand to undo Lana's pants, but she grabbed hold of it to stop him.

"Stop! Doug, this isn't right!" Lana proclaimed, but Doug continued.

Doug pinned her on the couch. She had nowhere to go. *No, no, not again,* memories of being molested flashed in her head, and this time, Cory wasn't there to save her. Closing her eyes, she felt tears building up and then Doug's body easing off of her. She opened her eyes and saw him standing still, shock written all over his face.

"I'm so sorry, Lana. I thought this was what you wanted."

A glance into Doug's eyes and Lana saw that his apology was sincere. Plus, she knew she was also to blame, and for a moment, she had wanted it.

"It's okay," she stuttered, "It wasn't entirely your fault."

Grabbing her bag, she sat across from Doug in complete silence. *How did I let this happen? Fuck, what am I going to tell Cory?* Lana thought. She looked at her phone and time couldn't move fast enough.

When she heard Cory pulling up into the driveway, she stormed out of the house. Like a madman, she opened the passenger door and slid into the front seat. Without looking at Cory, she said, "Let's go."

"What's wrong? What did he do?" Cory said, concern mingling with anger in his voice.

Lana placed her bag at her feet and kept quiet.

Cory undid his seatbelt and reached for the door handle. "I swear I'm going to smash his face in. I shouldn't have left you alone with him…!" Cory's temper went from 0 to 100 in a matter of seconds. Although he did not know why she was upset, he just naturally assumed Doug was to blame.

"No! Cory! Stop!" Lana yelled, drowning out his voice.

She leaned over Cory and forcefully pulled his seatbelt back on. She got up to pull his door closed.

"I want to go home, please, Cory. Just take me home," she pleaded, still looking away.

Cory had other things in mind – like hurting Doug.

At last, Lana turned to face Cory, with desperation in her voice, she pleaded once more, "Please, Cory, take me home."

Not wanting to upset her further, Cory complied, but intended to deal with Doug in the near future.

Lana's emotions were getting the best of her. Knowing she was about to cry, Lana turned away and stared out of the window as Cory drove off.

"Lana, um, you ain't gotta say anything, just listen. I don't know why you're upset, but I assume that it has something to do with Doug. How am I supposed to protect you if you don't tell me what happened?" Cory said as he drove onto the highway.

Odds were Lana would lock herself in his room when they got home and avoid him. This would be the best time to talk to her. But Lana didn't respond; instead, she shuffled in her seat, still looking out of the window.

"Come on, Lana, tell me what happened… please."

Lana turned to look at him; reaching to the dashboard of the car, she turned on the music, volume up to the maximum.

I can't leave her like this, and if that fool did anything to her…God help me, Cory thought.

He lowered the volume to talk again, not expecting her to answer.

"I want to apologize for before. I know I've shut you out more often than not, and I'm sorry for not always expressing myself to you," he said, glancing over to Lana to see if his words resonated. She was still gazing out the window. "Come on, Lana, I'm baring my soul here. You know how hard that is for me."

Still no response from Lana.

By now they had pulled into their garage. He spoke fast before she could open the car door and disappear into his room.

"Lana, I need you. I need you more than I need anyone else in my life right now. You keep me sane. I don't ever want you to pack up your things and leave - that would mean losing my sanity; it's why I reacted the way I did. I need you, Lana, and that hurts me so much to know it and admit it," Cory said, taking a deep breath.

Lana was looking out the passenger's window with tears running down her cheeks.

"Please don't cry, Lana, I don't want you to be sad anymore," Cory begged.

She turned to Cory, "Why couldn't you have told me that this morning, or yesterday, or all the other hundreds of times we've fought?"

To Cory, her voice sounded more regretful and sad than angry.

Looking into his eyes, she waited for an answer, but Cory was mute. Instead, he wiped away the tears streaming down her cheeks and caressed her face in such a delicate manner, that Lana's only response was to close her eyes and embrace Cory's soft touch. Without hesitating, he leaned over and pulled her face closer to his, kissing her forehead. A man with little words, but his actions spoke volumes, and it was the answer Lana had been waiting for. For the first time in a while, she felt his love and acceptance.

With traces of her tears still on his fingertips, he held her eyes with a tender look of admiration, then he leaned in and kissed her cheeks, letting his lips linger for a moment. His kisses felt like Kryptonite. He traced his lips up and down from her cheeks to her neck before kissing her passionately on her lips, causing Lana to let out a moan. She was weak and at the mercy of Cory's affection.

Tugging onto Lana's shirt, he pulled her closer toward him. This would lead to one thing, and she would be lying to herself if she said she didn't want it, but she couldn't go through with it. Using every ounce of strength she had, Lana pulled away from him, stopping Cory's advancement.

"I think we should go inside," she said, opening the door and walking through the garage to the back room of the house.

Oh my God! What am I doing? I just kissed Doug. Now I kissed Cory. This is so wrong, Lana thought as she walked through the house. She wanted nothing more than to pound her head into a wall, but she controlled her urge because she sensed Cory watching her every move. For now, she had to keep a poker face.

I can't tell him what happened, at least not now. Not after all he said...I didn't want to kiss Doug, it just happened. Fuck. All these damn technological advances and no one invented a time machine. Fuck!

She hurried to the bedroom to be alone with her thoughts.

"You're such a slut, Lana," she cried out. She had every right to be mad at herself for letting things escalate with Doug. It was out of character for her. Never in a million years would she have thought she would be the one to cheat in a relationship. *Things were so much easier when we were just friends*, she thought.

And she was right, things were simple when they didn't live together and all she had to worry about were the glares from every girl with a crush on Cory. But after The Sabbath, nothing was that simple anymore. Everybody's lives were ruined, and you were lucky if you had someone to keep you sane.

When Cory invited her to stay with him, she didn't hesitate for a minute. Over time, their relationship had grown to something more than just friendship, and with all the bad happening in the world, Lana shared some of her happiest moments with Cory. Now all they'd built together could be ruined by her single mistake.

She sat in the darkness of the room, beating herself up, too ashamed to even call her grandmother for advice. Her mind was in hyper-drive; she was so worried that with everything Cory had been through, and their past fights, telling him would mean losing him forever.

"I've got to tell him...the first chance I get," she told herself while playing out the anticipated conversation in her head.

Why did it have to be with Doug! Lana understood too well Cory's feeling about Doug. Had it been anyone else, Cory might be more understanding and willing to forgive. But with Doug, there was a chance that he would never forgive her.

Her body tensed. Cory was knocking on the door, waiting for her response.

"C-come inside, Cory," she said with her voice trembling.

Cory entered his room. He stood at the doorway for a moment, letting his eyes adjust to the darkness, then closed the door behind him. His mind was racing, trying to figure out what Lana was thinking. Terrified and confused as to what to do next, he just stood there.

"Are you all right, Lana?" he asked finally, hoping to get a response.

"Sit down, I need to tell you something," Lana replied.

He sat beside her on the bed and took her hand, but Lana pulled it back.

"What's wrong?" Cory implored.

Lana froze, unable to face her guilt. She couldn't bring herself to tell him, not when he was being so sweet to her. She trembled on the edge of the bed, sobbing like a child. Cory reached for her hand, and this time grabbed it with conviction.

"It's okay," he whispered, rubbing the middle of her hand in a circular motion while he stared at her.

Lana wiped away her tears and gazed at Cory. Cory's concern for her attracted her in ways she could barely imagine. The irony tearing Lana up inside was the affection she had been yearning for from Cory is coming at the moment she didn't deserve it. On one side, she wanted to confess, and on the other, she wanted him in the worst way.

At least let me have him one more time. She was wrong for thinking this, but Cory's soft touches overcame her.

They sat there, gazing at each other. Lana still wondered if this was the right thing to do, whilst Cory wanted nothing more than to put her fears to rest. Her eyes blazed with a fiery fervor that consumed Cory, making his body hot with passion. He peered deeply into her eyes as if seeking his own soul's reflection, and in that moment, he kissed her. A kiss full of vehemence, and Lana responded with the same heat.

Burdened with the fear of losing one another, neither one of them held back. Licking his lips, Cory inched closer to Lana. His movements: smooth and poetic - his eyes never wavering from her. To him, this moment made all the fighting and tension worth it, and he would not rush. Cory planned on taking his time exploring every inch of Lana's curvaceous body. Holding her by the waist, he picked her up and placed her in the center of the bed.

He lay on top of her now. She reached her face up to meet his and kissed him again. Each kiss left her breathless, drawing her in deeper as if he held her breath hostage. Most nights, his kisses were enough, but tonight she wanted more.

Her mistake with Doug grew fainter in her mind with every passing second. Her body craved Cory's touch, and it was time for her to have him. They spent the entire night entangled in sheets, making love until their strength departed.

*

Lying there in Cory's arms, guilt consumed Lana - now more than ever. She couldn't escape the torment of her betrayal and became a prisoner to her own thoughts. *I wonder what he's thinking. Should I tell him now?*

"Cory, we need—" she began, but Cory interrupted

"Babe, I know, but not right now. I don't want to risk ruining this moment."

Lana smiled at this. As much as she hated being told what to do, a part of her loved it when he took control. She climbed on top and kissed him. Their strength returned to them as they continued to make love, forgetting everything.

*

Lana turned her body to face Cory. Smiling, he used his hands to pull her in closer. He kissed her forehead as she lay on his chest, being rocked to sleep by the rhythm of his heartbeat.

"Cory, are you awake?" she whispered.

"Uh-huh, what's up?" he replied.

"Why can't you ever talk to me?" she said with her voice trembling. "It's okay if you don't want to answer, I don't want to fight...not right now."

"Babe...I wish I knew, sometimes I wish I can just run up to you and tell you everything, but I can't...it's the only way I know how to be strong."

"What do you mean?" Lana asked.

Cory sucked his teeth, "Well, when my dad left, I didn't understand why. I remember being so angry with everyone. My mom tried her best though, and for the longest, she was the one I ran to when I needed to talk."

He paused for a moment, then let out a big sigh and continued. "It was always the same: we would cry, she would hold me tight and remind me that it wasn't my fault. Back then, it was what I really needed to hear…it was what I wanted to hear, and it was enough to pick me up until my next episode."

He took a deep breath as his guard dropped. Lana held him tighter.

"Until, one day, I broke down while she was at work. I had no one to run to but my uncle, who had been watching us at the time. He was a good guy, but not the best with kids. I remember going to him bawling, screaming, and shouting God knows what."

"How old were you?" Lana interjected.

"Maybe six. Anyways, he picked me up and literally shook the fear out of me. He looked me straight in the eye and said, 'Cory, stop your crying! You gonna cry forever? Look at your sister - you think she's crying because of you or your dad? You're the man of the house now; you have to be strong for them.' Ever since that day, I stopped going to my mom with my problems. I saw her cry less, and even my sister didn't cry as much."

"He shouldn't have done that," Lana rebuked, shaking her head. "You were only six. Of course you would act that way."

"It's funny; at times, his voice still rings in the back of my head. I promised myself that I would put no one in a position where they felt sorry for me ever again. Lana, I'm the last person you should waste your tears on. When you've bottled everything up for so long, you forget how to let it out, and that's not fair to you or anybody else."

Lana had no response but to hold him tighter. But the ghost of her guilt returned to haunt her, depriving her of her sleep. She had to tell Cory what had happened with Doug. It wasn't a secret she could keep; Doug wouldn't let her keep it secret.

Either she told him, or Doug would. *Fuck!* She tightened her grasp on Cory. All she wanted to do was bottle up the feeling of his body on hers, just in case this was the last time she ever got the chance to be this close to him again.

13

Isabel pushed open the door.

"Cory," she called, trying to wake him, "the old man is at the door looking for you."

"What?" Cory responded, still half-asleep.

Isabel repeated it until Cory registered what she was telling him.

"All right, tell him to come inside. And close my door. Let me get dressed," he ordered.

"Okay, but hurry. I have no business entertaining a homeless man," Isabel replied as she shut the door behind her.

Cory turned his head and saw Lana, still passed out from the night before.

"Lana," he called out, shaking her shoulder, "the old man is here. Get up and get dressed so we can talk to him."

"Go on ahead. I'll be out in a minute," she mumbled with eyes still shut, not moving a muscle.

Not wanting to waste any more time, Cory walked into the bathroom and made himself presentable before heading to the living room.

His sister sat across from the old man, who wore the same ripped jeans and dingy T-shirt as always. A torn book bag rested at his feet. Cory felt awkward. The man had never given him his name, so he had no idea what to call him, and he didn't want to disrespect him. He thought fast before making his presence known.

"How are you doing, Boss?" he said.

The old man got up and greeted Cory with a firm handshake, "Ah. All is well, son. I hope this isn't a bad time."

"Oh no, not at all," Cory replied.

"Good, cause this is the only time I've got," he joked.

Cory led him to the dining room table. They sat and stared at each other for a moment until Isabel broke the silence.

"Well, I'm off to my room. You holler at me if you need anything," she told Cory.

"No, stay. You might need to hear this," Cory replied as he looked back at the old man. "So what brings you here?"

Before he could answer, Lana came strolling in, wearing a white robe.

"Good morning, darling," the old man said. "Come join us at the round table."

Lana took her seat and the old man began explaining the reason for his visit.

"Yesterday we had some suspicious guys roaming our neighborhood."

"The guys in black!" Isabel interrupted.

"Yes, them," the old man continued, "You guys need to tell me what you guys did to bring them here."

"Whoa," Cory shouted. "What makes you think we brought them here?"

"Son, I don't know if you guys did or not. But here are the facts. They were looking for something or someone, and they snatched folks off the streets. You guys are next."

"And why us?" Isabel asked.

"I've been around those out in the streets for a long time now. And not one of them thinks of you guys as their own. You don't act like them, you don't look like them, and you especially don't live like them. I mean, look at your established home here with no broken glass or bullet holes. Now I'm warning you, one of those folks are going to rat on you for their own sake, so if you want my help, you better come clean."

Isabel sat there with a confused expression on her face, but Cory and Lana had an idea of what the old man was talking about. Cory got up from his chair and headed to the basement. When he came back, he was holding the device Lana had analyzed, along with the blueprint.

"Here. We took these from a government convoy," Cory said, handing the items over to the old man. "Oh, and it was also addressed to a man named Damian Phils."

Damian, Damian…why does that name sounds so familiar? Lana pondered.

She shot up from her seat. "Oh shoot! Wait, I got something," she said as she ran to fetch the folder Doug had given her yesterday.

"Here," she said as she tossed the folder on the table in front of the old man.

"Where did you get that?" Cory asked.

"Doug," she replied.

The old man sat there, overwhelmed with the things being presented to him. Letting out a huge sigh, he picked up the folder and skimmed through the documents inside. He had a focused look on his face, so in return, the others kept quiet. He picked up the blueprint while placing the folder back on the table. He analyzed it for a few minutes before placing it alongside the folder. At last, he picked up the device.

Holding it in his hands, he said, "What can you guys tell me about this?"

Cory waited for Lana to respond.

"Umm, well, not much, but there's a small computer chip inside the device. It's something biometric judging by the blueprint and the image inside of it. I think— "

"What image?" the old man interrupted.

"Well, there's an image of the sun, and inside the sun, there's another picture of a brain, and the blueprint is shaped like a brain too," Lana responded. "But other than that, there's nothing more that I can tell you. I tried running a diagnostic on it, but the encryption on it was impossible to crack."

The old man pressed on the side of the device and it popped open revealing the computer chip inside.

How'd he know where to press? Cory pondered, surprised at how familiar the old man seemed with the device. They sat there in silence, waiting for the man to speak.

The old man rubbed his hands together and said, to himself, "Ah, where should I begin?" He nodded his head. "Okay, listen up, and be careful who you share this information with. For the protection of wisdom is like the protection of money, and the advantage of knowledge is that wisdom preserves the life of him who has it…

"Awhile back, a company named IBM announced to the world that they were planning on building a new programming architecture for chips inspired by the human brain: a chip that can copy the brain's capacity for perception, action, and thought. In other words, it would be the first of its kind to think like human beings, but at a more superior rate. This made many people upset, and I couldn't blame them. Giving machines the ability to think is dangerous in its own accord."

Cory and Isabel exchanged confused looks.

"I don't get it," Isabel confessed.

"Wait, let me finish," the old man continued, "Anyway, in a public expo of their work, IBM showed their brain-inspired computer chip. The exposition was very impressive, but caused a lot of uproar, and in the end, more and more people protested this revolutionary computer chip, causing the company to stop their advancement.

"It looks like Dr. Phils continued their research and created this device you see before you. Some say that if this was inside a human brain, the computer chip would function as neurons and communicate with nerve fibers. It would replicate and improve the brain's ability to respond to biological sensors and the handling of huge amounts of data from numerous sources at once.

"For those who aren't following me, this chip in a human brain can sense, remember, and cause that individual to act depending on the situations at hand. Now, just as any other computer chip, it can be programmed, giving the programmer the ability to subconsciously influence the decisions we make in our daily lives."

"What do you mean? Are they trying to control us?" Isabel cried out.

"Not control you like robots, but at a subconscious level, yes. This is another way for them to control us," the old man replied.

"How? They can't just force this on us. No-one will line up to get this implanted in their head," Cory blurted out.

"Yeah, you're right," the old-timer nodded. "They will sell it to the public as being something convenient and needed. That way, they wouldn't have to force it on anyone. People will line up to get this implanted inside them without knowing its implications."

The old man surveyed the room at the fretful faces.

"This device is dangerous, and the Government will do anything to get it back. I'm willing to bet when you tried to break its encryption, the chip sent out a signal back to home base giving off the location of this area. You guys are lucky. That signal must have failed to give them your exact location, which would explain why you guys haven't been caught yet."

The old man reached into his bag, pulling out three bracelets and tossed them on the table.

"I don't have to tell y'all that your lives are in danger. These bracelets are durable and hard to take off. There's also a tracking chip inside, so if anyone of you goes missing we can find out your exact location. Also, I will take these items with me to do further research, and in return, I will share everything I discover."

Lana and Isabel looked at Cory to figure out if he would let the old man take their things. Cory nodded in approval as the old man slid the device, folder, and the blueprints into his bag. He swung his bag over his shoulders as he got up.

The old man tossed a card on the table. "Here. There's my number. If one of y'all do go missing, that's how you contact me," he said as he walked toward the door.

They all sat lost in their own thoughts, looking at the bracelets and a card with just numbers on it.

"Is he telling the truth?" Isabel spoke out.

"Yes, I remember Doug telling me that the device was supposed to go to every city and that there was just enough to match the population," Cory responded. "Here, put the bracelet on. I got to figure out what we're going to do next."

"We shouldn't have given him everything we had though, especially the folder. I didn't have time to look through it," Lana said.

"Really?" Cory asked. "I figured you would have. Oh well, at least we have more of those devices left...I don't know; I just feel like we can trust him."

"Okay, so what do we do now?" Isabel asked.

"Not sure...amp up the security. And until we know what we're dealing with, everyone is staying indoors," Cory suggested.

*

A few days went by with no sign of the mysterious men in black. Cory knew he couldn't keep them inside for much longer. Their blood was boiling - they all felt like prisoners in their own home. But Cory still wasn't sure if it was safe enough to leave. After all, you needed heavy artillery to breach their house, and a step outside was a step out of their fortress.

"I can't stay in here for a single minute, let alone another day," Isabel cried out.

"Isabel...we talked about this," Cory tried to reason with her.

"She's right. This is too much," Lana agreed with Isabel. "We haven't seen those guys in days. It's possible they were looking for something else and moved on."

"Nope. They're out there. I can feel it."

"You're over reacting again," Lana told Cory. "Maybe those guys weren't looking for us at all, and they were just after some guy in the neighborhood."

Cory was very analytical, and that was what attracted Lana to him. His ability to strategize and come up with complex plans had saved their lives more times than she could count. And although she believed everything the old man had said about the device, she thought Cory and he were just being paranoid about the men in black.

"Lana, as much as I want to agree with you, I can't. This is too important to be taken as a mere coincidence," Cory continued, "If what the old man said is true, and I think it is, then somebody knows we have this device and wants it back…"

Cory paused and scratched his chin. "But why haven't they come? The only reason must be not everyone in the Government knows about this computer chip. Only a select few do, and they're not trying to draw any more attention to themselves than they already have. But they're out there waiting for us."

He put his hands on Lana's shoulders and looked deep into her eyes. "And it makes sense too. There're so many different parties working for the Government, not everybody would sign off on something like this." He looked over at Isabel, took a step away from Lana and said, "Yeah, this whole thing, the missing people, the device… Just a select few know about it, and one of them is on the corner…"

Great, another conspiracy theory, Lana thought. She blamed the Government for the missing people as much as Cory did, but Cory was letting the old man control him. Lana wanted to find out the truth her own way. She didn't want Cory to trust in everything the old man said, seeing as they didn't know him at all - not even his name.

Isabel had been putting on her sneakers, and strutted for the door. "I've had it! I don't care anymore…I'm going for a run."

Cory jumped in front of her, "You're not going anywhere."

Isabel took a step back and froze. Her eyes hardened as she lifted her chin. Stabbing her finger at him, she barked, "Cory, you must've lost your goddamn mind! Thinking you can talk to me like that, let alone control me - you better do your best to remember who's older!"

Cory felt humbled at the sight of his sister's rage.

"Isabel, please, just stay indoors. They're out there watching us," he pleaded to his livid sister.

Lana sat back and watched the situation unfold. She figured Cory wouldn't let Isabel go, but she also expected Isabel to stand her ground and do whatever she wanted either way. She needed to defuse the situation quick before things got uglier.

Jumping between the two, she reasoned, "Hey! Calm down guys. How about this - Cory, how about if I go running with Isabel? That way we can look after each other. I'm pretty sure both of us can handle any scum that's out there."

Cory's lips twitched and he opened them and took in a deep breath. Then his lips closed into a hard line. He knew, short of tying her up, he couldn't stop Isabel from leaving. On the one hand, he didn't want Lana to go, either, but on the other, she had made a good point.

"All right, go with her, but you guys make sure to flash your guns at anyone who might cause you trouble," he instructed, stepping away from the door.

Lana left the room and returned with her running shoes and two holsters with handguns, and handed one to Isabel. They strapped the holsters around their waists as Cory escorted them out. Before closing the door, Cory scanned the streets for anyone suspicious. As he watched them move down the block, he pulled his mother's picture out of his wallet.

"I can't lose them too," he said.

He let out a sigh and went back inside. Something wasn't right. He had a nasty feeling he would soon regret letting the girls leave their home.

14

Isabel and Lana started running as soon as their feet touched the concrete. Isabel led them into the park, where they jogged for fifteen minutes until Lana couldn't take it anymore.

"Stop!" Lana pleaded with her hands stuck to her knees.

Isabel was running ahead when she heard her. She jogged back to find Lana bent over trying to catch her breath.

"I take it, it's been a while," she joked, patting Lana on the back as she laughed.

"Ha! Yeah, I had no idea you were in great shape like this. You should meet my grandmother," Lana replied, still trying to catch her breath.

"What, she runs too?"

"Every day."

"Wow, good for her! This should be fine for today. Let's head back."

"Okay, but can we walk first? At least for a little while, my legs can't take it," Lana asked.

"Hahaha! Yes, we can."

They walked back, talking and laughing about anything that crossed their mind. More importantly, Lana could answer all the questions Isabel had about the device and their first conversation with the old man. It was the first time Lana had felt close to Isabel since The Sabbath.

"You really do care about my brother, don't you?" Isabel asked.

"Yes, but he's so freaking stubborn!" Lana replied.

"Trust me, girl, I know. Try living with him for nineteen years." Isabel said, laughing. "But in all honesty, he cares about you too; he just doesn't know how to express it… he's been through a lot."

"Yeah? But how about you, though, didn't you go through the same things?"

"Meh, I did, but it was different. I had outlets to relieve my frustration, and he didn't. I kinda blame that on my uncle, but that's another story. Anyways, they treated us differently."

"How so?" Lana asked.

"Well, whenever I got upset, they would console me - but when Cory showed any emotion, he got the, 'Stop. You're the man of the house' speech. So, soon enough, he stopped expressing himself altogether. When he was happy, he was happy; but when he got sad, he would disappear somewhere and come back when he seemed happy again."

"How was he when he found out about your mother's cancer?"

"Umm. It was a different reaction to what I was used to. Cory was quiet about the whole thing. He just locked himself in his room for days and only came out to eat. Then, once he got over the news, he started talking again."

"Really?"

"Yup. Hurt, disappointment, betrayal or any other emotions along those lines are hard for him to express. Usually, he'll just channel those emotions into anger but for this, he just went cold. But he was always there though. I remember when the burden of losing my mother was too much; I would run into his arms and just collapse there. He'd comfort me and tell me everything would be all right. When I had calmed down, he would go off to his room again." Isabel knitted her eyebrows into a frown, "Wow. I've never even bothered to ask him how he was holding up. What a big sister I am...Lana, thank you."

"For what?"

"For being there for him - for being good to him. He deserves it. I know it's hard, but please be patient with him. He suppresses a lot of emotions. The funny thing is, the last time I remember seeing him cry was the day our mom went missing."

Lana had an ache in her chest; the conversation saddened her. *He cried when we fought.* Guilt consumed her. *All I wanted was for him to show me he cared, and he was doing it right before my eyes. And I go out and kiss Doug? Ughhh! I'm so stupid!*

"Hey, are you all right?" Isabel asked, disrupting Lana's thoughts.

"Yes, I'm fine."

"Good," Isabel nodded. "Lana, why did you stay with us when your grandmother lives inside the walls? I've been meaning to ask you this for a long time now, and I totally get it if you don't want to answer."

"No, it's all right," Lana said, flashing a shy smile. "Well, my grandma always said when you start doing things that don't make sense then it's love."

"She's a smart lady," Isabel said, laughing.

Lana gripped the edged of her shirt and twirled it between her fingers. She kept her head down as she spoke.

"In all honesty, I've asked myself that question before and the simple answer is...I love him. He's flawed, but he is the best man I know. The way he protects me, protect us, I'm not going to find that type of love inside the walls. Besides, I don't want to live within a lie, shielded by the same people that might be responsible for your mother's disappearance."

"I understand and I'm so happy you stayed with us," Isabel said, stretching her arms and pulling Lana closer. "Now, are you ready to run back home?"

They ran down the sidewalk. They were three blocks away from home when, out of nowhere; an unmarked milky van screeched past them and stopped. The back door flung open as two white men dressed in black hopped out. Isabel wasted no time turning around and pushing Lana to do the same.

"Run," she screamed as they took off in the opposite direction.

Fueled with adrenaline, Lana forgot how tired her legs were. She looked behind her and saw the men chasing them. Isabel ran ahead without looking back; she made a sharp right turn into an alleyway. Lana made a sharp left and took cover behind an old car parked along the sidewalk.

I'll just slow her down, she thought as she drew out her gun.

She poked her head around the car to aim. She took a deep breath as she squeezed the trigger. The bullet exploded with a flash and entered the head of the man running in front. He dropped as his partner took refuge behind a parked car along the sidewalk.

Gunfire kept Lana pinned down. Two more men hopped out and charged toward her. She managed to hit one of them before shots forced her once again behind the car. Things weren't looking good. With little ammunition and no idea of who was after her, Lana's chance of survival dwindled by the minute. Still, she accepted her fate if it meant Isabel's safety.

The firing ceased. Peering from behind the car, she held her gun aim ready as she waited for a clear shot. Someone pushed her back behind the car.

"Isabel?" she yelped. "What are you doing here? No, no, no. Why did you come back?"

"I won't let them take you…not on my watch…not again," Isabel replied as she drew out her weapon. "Take that alleyway to the other side, make a right and keep running until you see our backyard."

Isabel fired two shots at their pursuers.

"Go, I'll cover you!" she ordered, but Lana refused to leave her. "Don't worry, I'll be right behind you."

Lana bolted into the alleyway, dodging the barrage of bullets flying at her. Once across, she turned and waved at Isabel to follow.

"Cover me!" Isabel said.

Lana stuck her hand out around the building and fired shots. One of the men tried to get closer, and she shot him in the neck -but that was after he had let off a shot that struck Isabel as she ran toward the alleyway.

Isabel fell to the ground, holding onto her right thigh. She roared in agony as she crawled back to the relative safety of the car. Thinking the worst, tears streamed down Lana's cheeks as she ran back to the car, untouched.

"Isabel, are you all right?" she screamed.

Isabel was squirming in pain. She mustered all of her energy just to talk.

"No, it's my leg. I can't run. Go!" she said, pushing Lana away.

"No!" Lana replied, choking back tears. "I'm not leaving you here - not like this."

Grabbing Lana's shirt, Isabel pulled her closer, "Leave your gun and run, I'll cover you. Go and tell Cory, he'll find me. Now go. Go!"

Lana laid her gun on the ground and bolted once more into the alleyway. She looked back and saw Isabel on her stomach, shooting at anything that moved. She ran until she was in front of their neighbor's abandoned house. She crossed the yard and hopped the fence, landing in their backyard. Running up to the patio, she placed her thumb on the electronic scanner, unlocking the back door. Yanking the door open, she threw herself inside, pushing the door shut behind her.

Lana was safe, for now...

15

"Cory," Lana yelled at the top of her lungs.

"What? What is it?" Cory said, running toward her. "Where's Isabel?"

Lana was breathless and too overwhelmed with emotions to talk, but when Cory realized that Isabel wasn't with her, she didn't have to say a word. Cory hurried to the cellar and came out holding an M16 rifle, and an extra magazine tucked inside his back pocket. He grabbed Lana's arms as he said, "Quick, take me to her!"

They stormed out of the house and got into the old Nissan. Cory sped down several blocks, before Lana ordered him to stop. A faint smell of burnt powder mixed with blood lingered in the air. Cory could already see the bullet holes that had ripped through the vehicles parked along the sidewalk.

Bursting out of the car, Lana ran to where she had left Isabel. She pulled her hands over her mouth as she broke down.

Cory came running up behind Lana, not aware of the situation. He placed his gun on the ground as he knelt down to console her.

"Lana, talk to me... where's Isabel?"

Lana tried to speak, but she couldn't. She was crying so hard that she struggled to breathe. She pointed down at the pavement. Cory stood up in disbelief. He shook his head at the trail of blood that vanished a few feet away from the car.

"No! No! Lana, tell me that's not Bell's blood!" he said, his voice cracking more with each word. She was too distressed to respond, so Cory asked again.

"Lana! Look at me! Tell me that's not Isabel's blood on the pavement?"

Lana did nothing but nod.

"No! No! No! No! No!" Cory cried, shaking uncontrollably.

He took two steps backwards and stumbled to the ground like a drunkard. "Not again," he screamed.

He began to hyperventilate. As soon as Lana noticed, she crawled over and held him. His body was rigid, and his breathing control wasn't returning to him anytime soon. Cory broke free of Lana's grasp and wobbled toward the car - but after a few steps, he stumbled back to the ground and vomited on the pavement. Exhausted, he rolled over onto his back, gasping for air as his head swayed from side to side. Lana clamped his head between her thighs. He stared up at her face as she cried and pleaded, "Breathe, Cory, breathe." Her voice became fainter with each second until he blacked out.

*

When Cory regained consciousness, he was lying on the couch. The first thing he noticed was Lana arched over him, holding onto his hand. Discombobulated, he tried to piece together what had happened. The memory of losing Isabel hit him like a train wreck, and anxiety returned with a vengeance. Lana saw this, and jumped on top of him.

"Cory, look at me, you gotta breathe!" she instructed.

This time, Cory managed to calm down, keeping his composure.

"Tell me what happened," he commanded.

Lana explained in detail the events that led up to his sister's disappearance. Tears ran down his face. The initial shock of losing his sister was gone, but now he had to deal with the reality. Without a word, he stood and went into his room, locking the door behind her. He needed to be alone. His emotions made him unstable, and in his present state, he felt it wasn't safe for Lana to be around him.

That didn't matter to Lana. She kept banging on the door, pleading to be let in, but he ignored her. The twin burdens of losing his mother and sister were unbearable; and it was time to face his demons. It was his time to vent his frustration in the only way he knew how. In his fury, he screamed, kicked, and punched anything he could get a hold of.

The weight of the world was on his shoulders, and he had no one to blame for Isabel's abduction but himself. He knew he shouldn't have let them go running while his gut was telling him otherwise. A full hour passed before he opened the door.

Lana walked into the room open-mouthed. The bed was flipped. Everything else was on the floor or broken, and there were so many holes through the wall; it reminded her of a scantron answer sheet from school.

She sobbed, fearful that Cory's act of aggression had been meant for her. She flew into his arms.

"Please don't hate me," she kept repeating.

Cory only blamed himself for Isabel's disappearance. Plus, deep down, he was proud that Lana had tried to sacrifice herself for Isabel, and even more proud that Isabel had come back for Lana.

"I'm going to get her back," he said, gently pushing Lana away.

Pulling out his phone, he dialed the old man's number.

"Talk to me," the geezer answered.

"Hello, this is Cory. I need your help."

"Say no more, wait by your phone. I'll send you the address where we can meet."

After a few minutes, Cory received a text of an address and instructions to pack their things. It was eight o'clock in the evening, and the old man expected Cory to be there no later than ten. Cory and Lana wasted no time getting ready. They left the house carrying just one suitcase full of clothes, which they tossed in the back seat of their Audi A5.

Going back inside, they retrieved their metal gun cases, along with their bulletproof vests. Popping the trunk open, Cory placed the gun cases on top of each other and threw the vests inside. Just when he was about to close the trunk, he remembered he'd forgotten the box filled with the devices. He ran back into the house as Lana waited in the car. Once everything was packed and loaded, he closed the trunk then climbed into the driver's seat.

"Did you finish setting up the security?" Cory asked.

"Yes, all the live feed can be accessed directly from our phones, and it will notify us via e-mail of any intrusion," Lana replied.

"Are all the doors locked?"

"It's telling me that everything is locked," Lana said, looking at her phone.

"All right, we're all set."

"Do you need to GPS where we're going?" Lana asked.

"Nah."

Opening the garage door, they peeled off into the streets. Cory sped down the lonely highway without saying a word. Lana expected as much and respected his space. Now wasn't the time for her to be asking Cory to express himself. Reclining her seat, she tried to take comfort in the silence. Everything had happened so fast, and just like Cory, she too needed time to herself. Isabel's face tormented her thoughts - telling her to run, over and over again - until a teardrop rolled down Lana's cheek like water on a leaf. Before long, she fell asleep to the sound of the soft music playing in the background. It wasn't long before the slowing of the car awakened her.

"Where are we?" she asked as she opened her eyes. Bewildered by her surroundings, Lana sat up and bellowed, "Cory, what are we doing here?"

Before he could answer, Lana asked again.

"Why are we at Doug's house?" This time, she waited for his response.

"Lana, I don't have time to argue. Go inside, call your grandmother and make arrangements to get out of here first thing in the morning," he replied, avoiding her question.

In protest, Lana folded her arms across her chest and reclined back in her seat, "Unless you drag me out of this car, I'm not leaving."

"Lana…I don't have time for this."

Adamant, Lana sat still, looking straight through the windshield, refusing to respond to Cory's plea. Picking a tree, she vowed to stare at it until they left.

"You'll be safer with your grandmother. That's where you belong," Cory continued.

Again, no response. She remained still and unmoved.

"This isn't your fight, and I can't afford for you to get hurt. I already lost my mom and sister. Lana, get out!" Cory howled.

Waiting for Lana to respond grew tiresome. Cory was perplexed: Lana would argue with him all the time, but now she had gone mute. With no patience for Lana's stubbornness, he unbuckled his seat belt, leant over to her side and pushed the passenger door open with his fingertips.

Lana responded by grabbing the door and slamming it shut.

Cory got out of the car and stormed over to the passenger side. He guessed he would have to drag her out after all. Just as he reached for the door handle, he heard Doug stepping outside.

"Hey, did we have plans for fixing up my security today?" Doug asked, walking over.

"Um, nah," Cory said awkwardly.

In his head, the plan seemed perfect—leave Lana with Doug and go save Isabel. He had forgotten how upset Lana was the last time he left her there. But seeing Doug brought back the memories. Now he didn't trust Doug as much as he did two minutes ago when he'd tried convincing Lana to stay with him.

"So why are you here?" Doug asked, confused and slightly hostile.

"Um, uh—I was going to drop Lana here for the night. She needs to go home to her grandmother tomorrow. I have some....stuff I need to handle, and I don't want her in it," Cory sputtered, regretting the fact that he had to depend on Doug.

"It doesn't look like she wants to be here," Doug replied, jaws clenched as if he had a bad taste in his mouth.

Taking a deep breath, Cory tried opening the passenger door. It was locked. He glared down at Lana, who was still looking out the windshield at the same spot.

"Lana, stop this bullshit. Open the door!" he demanded.

Lana seemed undeterred. Cursing under his breath, Cory walked back to the driver's side and removed the keys from the ignition. Now she couldn't lock him out. Striding back to Lana's side, he opened the car door and stepped aside to give her room. Doug stood back and watched to see what would happen. Nothing, she didn't move.

"You two are like a fucking soap opera, aren't y'all," Doug added with a frustration. "This is just another rejection, isn't it? Lana and her fucking games, I'm over this," Doug declaimed, walking back to his veranda. He stopped and called out, "If Lana is staying, the door will be open, but I'm not waiting to see what happens."

Cory wasn't sure what games he was talking about, but he had little time to inquire.

"Lana, get out of the car!"

Lana leaned over, glaring at Cory. Her eyes watered as she screamed, "You've insulted me for the last fucking time, Cory. I'm not getting out this fucking car. You're not doing this to me; you're not blocking me out. No, not this time! It's my choice, not yours. Fuck you, Cory. *Fuck you*! I'm not staying with punk-ass Doug and I'm going to find Isabel—because I'm more than capable of doing it. Ask me to get out of the car one more time and see how far I'll go to make you understand."

She slammed the car door shut, crossing her arms across her chest again.

Cory stood still, shock written over his face. He threw his hands up in defeat and climbed back into the driver's seat. Without saying a word, he reversed the car out of Doug's driveway and sped down the narrow country road. As they reached the highway, he pulled out his phone to give Lana an address.

"Pull that up on the GPS," he instructed.

They drove to an abandoned parking lot. There was no one at the rendezvous point, so they messaged the old man, notifying him of their arrival. They got out of the car and waited. Soon they heard a car engine approaching. They hoped it was the old man. Around the corner came a white Mercedes Benz G wagon speeding toward them. The car made a wide turn, pulling up beside them. The door opened and out came the old man. He was sporting a black tailored suit with a white dress shirt tucked underneath. The shirt's top buttons were undone revealing his hairy chest. Cory and Lana were too focused on Isabel to question the old man on his stunning change of appearance and the unexpected flashy entrance.

Their meeting was brief. They didn't have to say much. Isabel's absence alone gave the old man all the confirmation he needed to know that she had gone missing.

"Did she have on the bracelet?" the old man asked.

"Yes," Lana responded.

"Okay, well let's go find her then. You guys follow me," the old man instructed them.

Turning around, the old man started toward his car, but stopped and turned to point at Cory.

"The name's Bienaimé, and I promise I will do everything within my power to get your sister back."

His vow gave Cory and Lana a little more faith they could find Isabel. They shook hands before following him out.

Bienaimé led them to a dirt trail in the middle of the wilderness. The road was long and narrow with nothing but trees, reminiscent of Doug's home. It was quiet, and it didn't seem anyone would dare venture out there. Bienaimé made a sudden left turn off the road and into the woods. Cory followed and was surprised to find they had merged with another road, which had been hidden in plain sight.

Bienaimé decreased his speed. The terrain was a lot more rugged and narrower than the previous road. They drove up to what appeared to be a castle. It was the most beautiful work of architecture that Cory and Lana had ever seen. They stared in awe at the three-story, red brick home. It had more windows than they could count, and the entrance had two gigantic wooden doors with golden doorknobs, complimented by an arching roof. A triple garage was attached to the side of the house. Cory followed the old man inside the middle garage door.

Wow! This garage is bigger than my whole house! Cory thought, stepping out of his car.

"Leave your luggage inside, we will unload them later," the old man yelled from his vehicle.

"All right, but I have a box full of those devices in the car," Cory hollered back.

"Oh, you have more? Yeah, yeah, leave them too, we'll handle all that later," Bienaimé said, stepping out of his car.

"Is all of this yours?" Cory asked.

Bienaimé chuckled, "I hope this isn't too much for you, son."

"Why are you out on the streets every day dressed like a bum if you have all of this?" Cory continued with his questioning.

"Well, son, I dress like that so the people that want me killed will overlook me. To them, I'm just another old bum out on the streets, and I am of little threat to them. The irony is that those I'm seeking overlook me as well. I bet if I had on what I'm wearing right now out on those streets, more people would take me seriously."

Cory and Lana nodded.

"And your name—Bienaimé…is it French?" Lana asked.

"Well, aren't you the clever one. Yes, it is. It means beloved, given to me by my late grandfather," Bienaimé said, leading them through the garage door and into his home.

The mansion's breath-taking beauty again dazzled Cory and Lana. It was as though no walls existed. The open floor plan gave them a full view of the living room, kitchen, and dining area. A giant crystal chandelier hung above the dining table, attached to a vaulted ceiling that dwarfed even the tallest of men.

The kitchen had state-of-the-art stainless steel appliances and a full-length overhead ventilation hood that was worthy of the finest restaurants.

They moved to the living room area, and Bienaimé motioned to two crisp, white leather couches on a gorgeous round, creamed-colored Italian rug that softened the hardwood flooring.

"You guys want some water?" Bienaimé asked, walking toward the kitchen sink in the middle of the long white Carrera marble countertop.

"Yeah, if you could afford it," Cory joked, while Lana stood mute, shocked at the thought of drinking water still coming from a tap.

"Take a seat on the couch there."

"Hey, before we get too comfortable, is it possible to find out about my sister's whereabouts first?" Cory asked.

He didn't want to relax when Isabel's life was at stake.

"Yeah, yeah, of course, son. We'll get onto that right away," Bienaimé replied.

Bienaimé walked to the brown spiral staircase leading to the upper levels of the home, and called out, "Destiny! Adam! Come downstairs, we have guests!"

Soon, they heard footsteps walking down.

"Hello, Professor," said a casually dressed young man, standing on the landing above.

He was no older than Cory and of average height. He was a handsome fellow, with soft features that made his face forgettable. His physique was nothing special either. He was thin, yet had a toned, slightly muscular build. His brunette hair was the one thing memorable about him. He wore it short, and the top was slickly combed to one side.

"I keep telling him to stop with all this formality. Now, come down here and introduce ya'll selves," Bienaimé said.

The man met Cory and Lana at the bottom of the stairs. His personality at once atoned for any lack of distinct facial features. His movements were bold, walking with his head held high and shoulders straight. With grace, he shook Cory's hand with a grip that only a man with confidence possessed.

"Nice to meet you. My name is Adam Bell," he introduced himself to the couple with a southern accent. His voice was as powerful as a lion's roar.

He stepped aside for a young lady holding her hand out. "Hi, I'm Destiny. It's a pleasure to meet you guys," she said, shaking Cory and Lana's outstretched hands.

Unlike Adam, she didn't have to say much to make her presence felt.

She had a certain glow that would light up even the darkest of rooms; her beauty would make any woman feel intimidated. Her long, golden, wavy hair was pinned up, and she had big blue eyes as deep and wide as the ocean. With full lips the color of a red rose, her smile was pure and full of joy - enough to cast away any bitterness in one's heart.

"Adam and Destiny here are my pride and joy. Adam was my teaching assistant. He's a genius - the way he can speak with computers. Destiny's father and I served in the army together, and when he passed…God rest his soul, I took her in, and I've been blessed ever since. Her skills with a gun are unmatched. Well, enough with the introductions, let's get things started," Bienaimé said.

With their eyebrows up and curved, Adam and Destiny exchange looks. It was obvious they didn't know what Bienaimé was referring to when he said, "let's get things started," and appeared curious as to why he had brought strangers into their home.

Bienaimé looked at Adam and said, "Son, please escort our guests to the basement. I will explain everything there."

Adam didn't hesitate. He led them past the marble fireplace and a black grand piano, to a closet door nestled between two of the many rich, abstract paintings that decorated the creamed colored walls, near the main entrance of the house. The closet was filled with jackets and coats. Stepping inside, he pressed a button, and the back wall slid to the left, revealing a hidden staircase. They walked down to the basement.

Cory and Lana stood in amazement. The walls were neatly lined with Grade A military weapons and accessories. A round table that could seat twenty people, and a high-tech computer was stationed in the middle of the room, along with other equipment and machinery that Cory or Lana had never seen. Bienaimé joined them, and guided Adam to the computer, where he took a seat as they all stood back and watched.

"Son, to cut a long story short, Cory's sister is missing. She was wearing the bracelet, and I need you to track her location for me," Bienaimé told Adam.

Adam wasted no time. In an instant, he was busy typing on his keyboard as Cory and Lana watched. He pulled up a map with a flashing beacon in the corner and projected the image onto the white wall.

"Professor, it's the same location as the others," Adam informed with a straight face.

"Sorry," Cory interjected, "what do you mean by 'it's the same location as the others?'"

Bienaimé answered, "The location where your sister is being held is the same place we've been investigating for months now. Years ago, it used to be an old prison. But shortly before The Sabbath, the Government emptied the inmates out and converted the premises into a research facility. We have reason to believe that the Government is using the same prison to keep the missing people captive, while conducting their research. And now, your sister is there too. That means that there's a connection between the device and The Sabbath."

"Oh, so they're the ones who gave you the device," Destiny said, pointing to Cory and Lana.

"Yes, and now their sister is missing," Bienaimé replied.

"So, that's where they're keeping everybody that went missing? How big is the prison?" Lana asked.

"No darling, not everyone." Bienaimé replied. "Just the people in the surrounding area. There's got to be hundreds of these facilities, if not thousands, all over the world."

"How far is it?" Cory asked. The thought of holding both his sister and mother again consumed him, and he wanted to act as soon as possible.

"About an hour's drive, tops!" Adam replied.

"Where is it exactly?" Cory asked.

"It's a—" Adam began, but was cut off by a roar from Bienaimé.

"Don't give it to him!" Bienaimé interjected, "Now, son, I know what you're thinking. But we need more time, more information. We can't just march over there and start shooting things up if we are not prepared for the consequences. You're not the only one going through the motions; there are two other people in this room who have their loved ones in that prison."

Bienaimé placed his hand on Cory's shoulder and continued, "Now, I told you before that I will do whatever I can to get your sister back, so let me do that. I can't risk you ruining months of research because you weren't prepared…my people are destroyed from lack of knowledge. Give me a week, and then we will act."

Cory wanted nothing better than to run to his car and get his family back, but he knew Bienaimé was right. If he went after them unprepared, chances are he'd be captured too. For the time being, he had no choice but to once again put his trust in the old man and hope he'd make good on his promise. One thing was certain, he was not going back home without his sister and mother.

"Okay, so what do you suggest we do?" Cory asked.

"Adam, can you please pull up the doctor's picture?" Bienaimé said.

Adam toggled through files and within seconds an old man's mug shot appeared on the wall.

"This man you see before you is none other than Doctor Damian Phillips, also known as Dr. Phils," Bienaimé said, pointing at the picture. "I used to work with him, and when I found out what he and the Government were up to…well let's just say we went our separate ways.

"For the past month, we've had sightings of Dr. Phils near the same place they are keeping your sister. He is usually there to welcome the convoys, and then he disappears into the building. I believe the device you gave me was supposed to go there. Now Cory, the box that is in your car - was that all there is?"

"No, there was a lot more in the truck, more than I could count," Cory answered.

"And you got this from Doug, I'm assuming," Bienaimé said.

"Yeah," Cory and Lana echoed.

"Listen up," Bienaimé said, waving his finger between Cory and Lana. "I already told you about how dangerous it is if it falls into the wrong hands, and it's evident they want it back…all of it. They can't risk people knowing about this so expect them to contact you to set up a trade. But let me tell you this: they have no intention of releasing your sister. In their eyes, she knows too much and as soon as you show up with the goods, you're done for.

"Now, Lana, the file you gave me contained Dr. Phils's personal files. It had nothing we hadn't already discovered, but it had his personal notes and handwritten signatures. If Doug got it for you, then that means he has access to Dr. Phils, and that's something we desperately need. That man might be the main reason why so many of our brothers and sisters are living outside the walls.

"So to answer your question, son, here's what we'll do. First: I need you to set up a meeting with Doug. We need to know where the other devices are, and we also need his assistance to kidnap Dr. Phils at the same time we rescue your sister. Second: Adam over there will schedule a meeting with my colleagues and get more firepower. And third: I need to see how good you guys are in the field before we do anything. I can't have you slowing us down."

"All of this and we will get them back in the course of a week?" Cory asked.

"Son, I said we will start to act in a week, and that act starts tomorrow with a meeting with Doug. Have faith, son. I know what I'm doing.'"

"Okay, I believe you. We'll set that meeting up right away," Cory said, nodding his head.

"Adam, see how many men we have available, and get them to meet us two days from now!" Bienaimé barked.

Again, Adam started typing on his keyboard and toggling through files.

"We have about twenty men available; the rest are on assignments. I will send out notifications now for the meeting. Oh, and Jeff just got back. He says he has news for you, so I will send him an invite as well," Adam said.

"Thank you, that's it for today. Adam, Destiny, if you could be so kind and help Cory and Lana with their things and show them to their room. Cory, can you leave that box with Adam? I will start dinner."

Cory and Lana went back to their car to grab their things before being escorted to their room.

"Sorry to hear about your sister," Destiny said to Cory as they climbed up the stairs. "But if anybody can get her back, it's Bienaimé."

"Oh, thank you. I appreciate it, and I plan on getting her back no matter what," Cory replied.

"Well, here's your room. If you guys need anything, just let us know. There's a bathroom in your room, and a game room on the third floor if you guys get bored. We'll let you settle in and I'll come get you guys for dinner," Adam explained as he opened the door.

They left the couple in the bedroom and headed back downstairs. Cory and Lana didn't bother to unpack; it made little sense to them, seeing as they weren't planning on staying long. They tossed their suitcase in the closet and jumped onto the bed.

"She's cute, isn't she?" Lana asked as she admired the room.

"Huh, what?" Cory pretended not to hear.

"Destiny, do you think she's cute?"

"Meh, she's all right," Cory said as he yawned.

"Just all right?" Lana continued.

"Yes, just all right. Don't tell me you're jealous now," Cory said and began to playfully grapple with Lana.

Lana giggled, "No, I'm just asking a question."

"Oh, well I couldn't care less how good she looks. I need to be focused," Cory said, pulling out his mother's picture.

Lana could tell just how anxious Cory was. He was confident he would at long last get his family back, and that made it easier for Lana to believe too. They laid there, optimistically talking about how their lives would soon change, until they were called for dinner.

That night, as they sat and ate, they exchanged stories and laughter, and were reminded of how things had been before The Sabbath. The nostalgic feeling was soothing, and Cory wished he could hang on to it forever. After dinner, they marched back up to their room. It had been a very long day, and they both needed rest – not to mention that after today...who knew when they would find sleep again.

16

Cory woke up the next morning to the sound of running water. He laid there staring at the ceiling, a bit apprehensive about what the day might bring. They were supposed to meet with Doug in a few hours, and he needed to know what had happened that night between Doug and Lana.

I wonder what Doug meant by Lana and her games? Man, all we do is argue, he thought.

"Wow, I haven't had a shower like that in like forever!" Lana rejoiced, stepping into the room and disrupting Cory's thoughts.

"Huh?" Cory said.

"Running water - it's like how it was before; you turn on the faucet and just relax," Lana smiled.

"Oh."

"What's wrong?" she asked, not liking his one worded response.

Cory paused for a moment, unsure of how he should frame his question. He shifted his stance upright with his back against the headboard.

"We need to talk, and no arguing - don't snap when I ask you this, just tell me the truth," Cory replied with caution. He watched as Lana stiffened her composure. The joy she had been experiencing from her shower faded.

"Okay, what is it?" she asked.

"What happened between you and Doug?"

"I don't..." Lana interrupted.

"Wait, let me finish," Cory said, raising his hand. "We're meeting him today. The last two times we met, it wasn't pleasant. Tell me what happened, so I don't go into this blind. We're supposed to be in this together. If there's something that will jeopardize me getting my family back, now is the time to say it."

Lana sat at the edge of the bed, with a huge cotton towel wrapped around her body. It was time to confess. She took the edge of the towel close to her knees and twirled it between her fingers.

"Well," Lana began, "It was like…I don't know how it happened. It just did. He was nice at first and funny. We were fighting. It seemed like you hated me. But after it happened, I felt so terrible. I started to hate myself; I always make stupid mistakes…"

"Lana, you're babbling. I'm barely following what you're saying." Cory said with his fists clenched, not liking the way she was talking.

Lana took a deep breath. Without looking in Cory's direction, she said it aloud, "Doug and I kissed. It was a mistake, and I stopped him. But I should have known better."

She bit her lips, waiting for Cory to snap and break the bed in two or throw something at the wall. But he just sat there, still, rested against the headboard.

Lana's betrayal sickened Cory deeply, causing the pit of his stomach to drop. He didn't know which was worse, the fact that she kissed Doug or the fact that she had sex with him right after. Whatever it was, he couldn't stand the sight of her.

I trusted this bitch, he thought.

No matter how hard he tried, he couldn't bring himself to hate Lana, but his hatred for Doug burned with a new passion. He'd always wanted to whip the smug smile off the man's face, and now he had a legitimate reason to do so. However, for his sister's sake, his anger must wait. Contemplating what to do next, Cory remained still.

Taking a deep breath, he responded, "Okay."

He then got up and walked toward the bathroom, but Lana jumped in front of him.

"Cory?" she said with sorrow, "Say something, anything. I know I should have told you before… please talk to me."

Not swayed by Lana's tears, Cory brushed her off and made his way to the bathroom, locking the door behind him.

Lana was shocked. She'd expected him to throw a fit inside, but all she heard was running water. There were no sounds of mirrors breaking or things being thrown about. This anger was new to Lana, and it scared her.

Cory never acts like this; his emotions always get the best of him. Oh my, he hates me.

Lana sat on the bed, sobbing like a baby. For all she knew, their relationship was over, and she couldn't bear it. She had known that sooner or later, the time would come where she would have to tell him, but she wasn't expecting Cory to react the way he did. Usually, he would lash out in anger, getting over it in time, but this time she got nothing out of him.

*

Walking out of the bathroom, Cory didn't utter a single word to Lana, who was still in her towel - too distraught to get dressed. Pacing over to the closet, he grabbed a set of clothes before returning to the bathroom. While looking back at Lana, who was still sitting, and before closing the bathroom door, he snarled, "Get dressed."

*

Cory led the way down the stairs as Lana trailed behind.

"Oh, good morning. There's some breakfast on the table. You two eat up. I'm gonna grab some things before we head out. I sent Destiny and Adam on an errand so it's just going to be us," Bienaimé said as he disappeared into another room.

Lana was grateful that Adam and Destiny weren't home and that Bienaimé was distracted. This way none of them could witness the current awkwardness between Cory and herself.

"Cory, talk to me," Lana pleaded from across the table.

Cory kept his head down and continued eating.

Lana was frustrated, but she had no one to blame but herself. All she could do at this point was to give Cory space and hope he would eventually forgive her.

"Okay, I'm ready to go now," Bienaimé said, coming from around the corner.

Taking their last bites, the two followed Bienaimé to the garage.

"Should we take my car?" Bienaimé offered.

"Yeah, sure," Cory replied.

They hopped into the Mercedes and drove to Doug's house. Upon their arrival, Cory advised Bienaimé to stay in the car.

"I'll wave at you to come after we explain who you are," Cory said, exiting the vehicle and walking toward the front porch. They were halfway to the door when out of nowhere, Doug stormed out of his house aiming a loaded shotgun at them.

"What the fuck is this? Who is that man in the car? You know better than to bring a stranger to my home!" he said, demanding an answer.

"Doug, put down the gun. The man in the car is our sponsor–" Lana tried to reason.

"I don't give a fuck who he is! I don't want him here," Doug shouted over Lana's voice.

"Chill for a second and listen to her. We're not about any bullshit right now," Cory interjected.

Lana continued where she had left off before Doug interrupted, "We didn't tell you that we were bringing him because you wouldn't agree to it. The upside is that he has lots of money and will do business with you. So you can either send us back on our way, or I can tell that man to come inside and we can talk."

Doug glanced at Cory, then over to Lana and remained silent for a moment. "Okay, bring him in," he said, distaste in his mouth.

Looking back, Cory waved and Bienaimé exited the car. They gathered in Doug's living room with hostility still lingering in the air.

"So, to whom do I owe the pleasure?" Doug said, glaring at Bienaimé.

"My name is not important, but what I can do for you is," Bienaimé replied.

"Then let me cut to the chase, what the fuck do you want?" Doug barked.

Cory glared at Doug in disgust. To Cory, nothing would be better than punching him in the face, and Doug's attitude toward Bienaimé intensified his urges. The only thing restraining him from attacking Doug was the thought of his mother and sister.

"All right, I'll be frank," Bienaimé said, pulling out the device. "Do you have any more of these?"

"Those? Yeah, I have a whole truck full of them. I have found no one willing to buy them, let alone anyone that knows what they are."

"Then I'm willing to take it off your hands. Name your price," Bienaimé said.

"How much are you willing to pay?" Doug asked.

"For a whole truck full, I'll give you twenty thousand," Bienaimé said in a hurry.

Doug's face lit up, "You got yourself a deal my friend!"

"Perfect, you can get in contact with Cory or Lana later to set up the exchange."

"Sounds good, and hey, if you ever need anything else, I'm your guy," Doug offered, noticeably more cheerful now.

"Well, that's great to hear, son, because there is one more thing I would like to discuss with you."

"Yes, go ahead," Doug replied.

"Are you familiar with a guy named Damian Phils?" Bienaimé asked.

"Yeah, what about him?"

"What is your relation with him?" Bienaimé asked, not answering Doug's previous question.

"We don't really have any relations to be honest. Sometimes I work as his personal guard, other times, I deliver inventories to him, and he signs off on it. Other than that, the guy is a complete stranger."

"All right, I need to bring him in for questioning, can you help?"

"You mean kidnapping? Whoa! I'm not sure about that!"

"I'll give you thirty thousand for your help, and I will make sure that it's done in a manner that looks like you were just doing your job."

Doug took a second to think, "Okay, thirty thousand, and if I can't go back to work, then that's a hundred thousand."

Looking at Cory and Lana, Bienaimé nodded, "Okay, we have a deal. Now all we need is some information from you so that we can come up with a perfect plan. You said you do deliveries for him, do you deliver things to that facility with the two big watch towers standing side by side near the entrance?"

"Near the old prison? Yes, I do. I'm scheduled to do a drop off there in a few days."

"What are you delivering?"

"Two backup generators, nothing worth taking."

"Okay, we will coordinate his kidnap with your delivery. I need you to think of everything possible about the set-up of the place. I mean from shift swaps, to how many men are on guard, and how they communicate. You will give me this information when I get my devices and you get your money," Bienaimé said as he got up, prompting everyone to rise from their seats.

"All right, as soon as I get your things together, I'll call you. Just get ready to meet me later tonight," Doug said, shaking Bienaimé's hand.

They left Doug's house and walked back to the car.

"Crazy world we live in when men are willing to kidnap a person they barely know for a few bucks. Whatever happened to do to others as you would have them do to you?" Bienaimé said, driving off.

Cory wasn't surprised at all by Doug's actions; Doug would sell his own soul if someone made him a good enough offer.

"All that guy cares about is money. I can't see how anybody could ever like a person like that," Cory said, taking a stab at Lana.

"Oh, you'll be surprised of what people are capable of," Bienaimé replied.

"Trust me, I'm starting to find out."

Lana knew exactly what Cory was implying, but kept quiet. She promised herself that she would let Cory vent out his frustration, plus she didn't want to say anything with Bienaimé in the car.

"All right, I'm going to drop you guys off with Adam and Destiny to do some training. I have to go and make sure everything is ready for the meeting tomorrow," Bienaimé explained, changing the subject.

They drove to an abandoned golf course, where Adam and Destiny had been waiting.

"Try not to kill each other," Bienaimé shouted from his car window as he drove off.

Maybe Cory and Lana should have taken that joke for a warning instead.

17

"Welcome to your training grounds," Destiny said with a smile.

"Before we begin, tell us - how did the meeting go?" Adam interjected.

"It went well. We're now waiting for Doug to contact us to go grab the other devices," Lana responded.

"That's good to hear. Looks like everything's on schedule then. Okay, let's start," Adam said.

Cory and Lana weren't too worried about the training exercise. They could take care of themselves. They were more excited to see what Adam and Destiny had in store for them.

"Okay, so we'll train you on your conditioning, shooting, and combat. Since there's little time, this is going to be relatively basic. Professor wants us to make sure that you guys can handle yourselves out there when the time comes." Adam glanced down at his watch. "Let's head out. I'll take Cory to do some conditioning and combat. Lana, you will stay with Destiny to do some shooting -then we'll switch up later. Are you ready to do some running, Cory?"

"Yup, let's go," Cory said.

The guys jogged away, leaving Lana and Destiny standing on the open green field.

"I guess we should get going too," Destiny said.

"I'm ready when you are," Lana replied.

Destiny guided Lana to the driving range. Its open grassland with its distance markers had golf balls, and several white mannequins positioned throughout, the closest mannequins being a few yards away and the furthest being a few hundred yards beyond that. The girls stood inside an individual stall with the view of the entire field. A table stood in front of them, jam-packed with ammunition, two handguns, M16s, M24 sniper rifles, two headsets and two safety glasses.

"You ever done any shooting before?" Destiny asked.

"Yes, I used to do it all the time," Lana replied.

"Great! Then this should be a breeze," Destiny said with a smiled. "All right, so first things first – on the table, you have your average 9-millimeter pistols, and the magazines are all empty. I need you to reload it for me."

Picking up a pistol, Lana could tell it was empty by its weight, but she pressed the mag release on the side of the frame to drop the magazine, and then pulled the slide back, locking it open and checked the chamber.

"I love the grip on this one," Lana said, placing the gun back on the table.

She shuffled through the ammunition until she found the nine-millimeter, then proceeded to fill the magazine. Picking up the pistol again, she smoothly re-inserted the magazine into the handgrip until she heard a clicking noise, and tapped it with her palm to make sure the magazine was seated. Before placing the gun back on the table, she flicked the safety on.

"Wow, you know your way around guns," Destiny noted.

"Told you I had lots of practice," Lana laughed.

"Ha! I believe you. Now it's time to do some actual shooting. I want you to pay attention to the mannequins I'm about to shoot, because after I'm done, I will ask you to do the same."

Destiny snatched a headset and safety glasses from the table before taking a couple of steps toward the open field. Pulling her gun from her holster, she disengaged the safety. Keeping a firm grip with her right hand, she pulled the slide back using her left, with a smooth and practiced movement, loading a round into the firing chamber. Re-establishing her two handed grip, she raised the muzzle, and acquired her first target.

Lana, who had put on a headset and glasses, walked a few paces closer to Destiny in order to see her shooting pattern.

Setting her jaw, Destiny began shooting, hitting her marks with precision while swinging her arms from side to side as she moved from one target to the next. As soon as she emptied her gun, she dropped the spent magazine to the ground and replaced it with another, all in a fluid motion. When she was done, she thumbed the safety back on, and re-holstered her gun. Walking back to the table, she grabbed a magazine and tossed it at

Lana.

"Here, this one is full. Put it somewhere you can have easy access to."

"Okay, gotcha!" Lana nodded, sliding the magazine underneath her belt and grabbing the loaded gun off the table.

"And when you're reloading, it should be second nature to you. You should never take your eyes off your target or have to lower you gun. Know where your magazine is and swap it instantly."

"Got it," Lana replied.

"Perfect. So I need you to shoot all those mannequins up until the fifty-yard mark. You can start whenever you're ready."

Lana was impressed with Destiny's shooting, but she viewed it as a challenge and wanted nothing better than to show her up. Taking a deep breath, she hit all the targets in the exact order Destiny had, and reloaded her gun with barely a pause in firing.

"Wow, you're just full of surprises! Where did you learn how to shoot like that?" Destiny asked.

"After The Sabbath, Cory forced me to learn how to shoot along with his sister. It bothered him leaving us at home with no protection."

"Oh, that was smart of him."

"Yeah. How about you?" Lana asked.

"Well, my dad was a general, and he taught me. While most kids were learning to ride bikes with their parents, he took me to the gun range."

She isn't so bad. She's kind of cool, Lana thought, realizing the many things they shared in common. Their fathers were both in the military, and they were both great shooters. They could become good friends if Lana allowed it...

"Okay, are you ready to try out the M16 now?" Destiny said.

"Yup, let's do it."

They grabbed the assault rifles and took turns firing at the mannequins.

"I needed that," Lana said, placing the powerful weapon back on the table.

"What?" Destiny said, confused as to what Lana was talking about.

"I needed this. I had to release my frustration somehow."

"Oh, girl, I know just what you mean. Every time I get frustrated, I come out here and shoot. You don't want to be here when you're too depressed though. Otherwise, you might end up shooting yourself," Destiny joked.

Lana laughed and then asked, "Question: why this golf course though?"

"It's owned by my uncle, Bienaimé. He told me that he bought it to spy on politicians. He always used to tell me: 'Darling, the most diabolical plans are discussed while playing golf.' After The Sabbath, we closed up shop and made it our own personal training ground."

"He's your uncle?"

"Yes. Well, not blood-related, but he was my dad's best friend, so he's been in my life since birth."

"Oh okay. I get it."

"Yeah, but tell me something about you. Are you and Cory an item? He's cute."

Cute?! Lana thought, lost on how to react to Destiny's comment. It was the first time in their relationship that she didn't feel secure about her position in his life. Girls complimenting him had never bothered her before, because they couldn't compete with her. Now she wasn't as confident. She believed Cory found Destiny attractive, and the Doug incident did nothing to help their relationship. Although Destiny meant no harm with her comment, Lana didn't know her well enough to trust her, and she wasn't willing to give her any ideas.

"Yes, we are. Are we going to shoot the sniper rifle as well?" she asked, changing the subject.

"Oh yeah, of course," Destiny replied, reverting her attention back to the training.

As soon as Lana reached for the weapon, her phone vibrated.

"Sorry, it's from Doug - he wants me to forward him Bienaimé's contact information, so they can meet up."

"Oh, no worries. Business first," Destiny said, waiting for Lana to finish replying to Doug's message.

"Okay, I'm all set," Lana said, inserting her phone back into her pocket.

Grabbing a box of match-grade ammunition and the sniper rifles, they took the gun and attached it to the bipod already stationed in the stall. While lying down on their stomachs, they took turns shooting at targets a few hundred yards away.

"Well, I think we're done here," Destiny said, realizing Lana hit every mannequin.

"Yeah, if this is how training is going to be, then sign me up!" Lana said as she placed the gun back on the table.

"Just make sure you tell Adam you had more fun with me," Destiny joked. "We should go now - it's almost time to do the switch."

They walked back to the rendezvous spot and waited for the boys to arrive. It wasn't long before they spotted two figures running toward them. They were sprinting neck-to-neck, when Adam used one hand to push Cory aside, causing him to lose his balance and slow down.

"Hey, you cheater," Cory yelled while chasing after him.

They both ran right past the girls before slowing down a few feet away. They hunched over with both hands placed on their knees, trying to catch their breath.

"You know we're gonna have to do that one again," Cory said, laughing.

"I'll see where I can schedule you in," Adam joked.

Cory and Adam both had their shirts wrapped around their heads, leaving their upper bodies exposed to the beating sun, sweat dripping down on their toned physiques. Lana tried not to stare at Cory, but failed. It was as if she was viewing him through a magnifying glass. She watched the sweat trickling down his shoulders, past his nipples and rolling over his rock-hard abs before disappearing into his shorts. *You're punishing me, aren't you God?* She glanced over at Destiny, and Destiny caught her gaze and returned it, with a wink. *Ugh, why Father? Why?* she cried to herself. The thought of leaving Cory alone with Destiny annoyed her, but at this point, there was nothing she could do.

"Don't worry about that, Cory - we all saw him cheat," Destiny said.

"Finally, somebody who is fair," Cory said, flailing his arms in the air.

"Are you ready to go, or do you need a few minutes to catch your breath?" Destiny asked Cory.

"No, I'm fine. Let's get going," Cory replied.

The two moved off, leaving Adam and Lana alone.

"Hey, are you all right?" Adam asked Lana with a concerned look on his face.

"Yes, I'm fine, just worried about getting his sister back," Lana lied. Although she was worried about Isabel, it was her jealously that was bothering her.

"Don't worry, we'll get them back," Adam said confidently. "Now are you ready to run?"

"Yeah, I am."

They jogged on a trail around the golf course until Adam abruptly stopped.

"Great pace, Lana, but are you ready to tackle that hill?" Adam said, pointing to a steep hill directly across from them.

"Ahh, you mean that mountain over there. I don't think so."

"Come on, it's a piece of cake," Adam said as they walked toward the base of the hill.

The hill rose a hundred meters from the base to the top.

"Okay, we're going to sprint to the top and walk back down then repeat for a total of ten times, got it?" Adam instructed.

"Got it!"

They sprinted to the top, the steep incline forcing them to use the balls of their feet. By the second ascent, Lana's legs felt much heavier. Like a champ, she pushed through the pain and ran up the hill six times before every muscle and nerve in her body screamed for her to stop. She highly doubted she would make it up the hill ten times. Looking up, she saw Adam at the top, waiting and clapping his hands in encouragement.

"Come on, Lana," he shouted, "Go your hardest, and we'll cut it down to eight instead of ten."

Her body was at the exhaustion point, but she couldn't pass up the opportunity to meet the challenge. She put all of her effort into forcing her leaden limbs to complete the last two climbs. When it was over, she collapsed on the ground with her back against the soft grass, and massaged her calf and thigh muscles.

"That was hell," she gasped, completely exhausted.

They laid there for a few minutes looking up at the clouds.

"All we need now is that perfect breeze," Adam said.

"Um-hm," Lana nodded. "Hey Adam, if you don't mind me asking, are you and Destiny a couple?"

Adam laughed, not sure how to respond.

"Me and Destiny? No, she's like my sister, I-we would never..."

"Oh," Lana said, disappointed, "well, I think you guys look cute together."

"Well, I thank you for your blessing, Miss! Now, are you ready to do some combat?" Adam asked.

"After what we just did? I don't know, Adam."

"Come on, now, there's water where we're going next."

"Water? I would do anything for a cup of water right now. Oh, Adam, you sure know how to bribe a lady," Lana teased.

"Ha ha, come on!" he said, helping Lana to her feet.

*

Meanwhile, at the opposite side of the golf course, Destiny had finished demonstrating her shooting technique and what she expected Cory to replicate.

"Lana told me you had her and your sister learn all about guns. I hope you're just as impressive as she is," Destiny teased.

"Yeah, I taught her everything she knows, but she kind of excelled and became a better marksman than me."

Although their relationship was rocky, Lana wasn't around, so he gave her due credit.

"But don't think for a second I'm not good competition. I hit my targets," Cory added, picking up a pistol. He examined the handgun as he tucked a spare loaded magazine in the left side of his holster belt. Having a conversation revolving around Lana bothered him, so he shifted the focus back to his training.

"Can I start?" he asked, looking back at Destiny.

"Uh sure…whenever you're ready," Destiny replied.

With his shirt still off, Cory caught Destiny ogling his frame. As he aimed, he smiled coyly, imagining the horror Lana would feel knowing Destiny might be her biggest threat yet.

*

"Okay, your goal right now is defense. Focus on protecting yourself. When you don't have a gun with you. What will you do then?" Adam instructed Lana.

They were in a spacious room of the golf course lodge. It was empty except for a few punching bags and mats spread over the floor. The walls were made of glass. From inside, Lana could see much of the golf course, as well as the dining area inside the lodge.

"You know, Adam, this style of fighting isn't for me. I'm the kind of girl who prefers to punch you in the throat, and while you topple over and cry, I'll run away or shoot you."

"We'll get to that, Lana," Adam said, laughing. "But first, I need to make sure you can defend yourself from attacks where you can't punch someone in their throat."

Lana was happy she could joke and poke fun with Adam. She was weary of being sad and Cory's silent ridicule of her every move.

"Okay, Lana, so what do you do if someone much bigger than you grabs you from behind?" Adam said, creeping up behind Lana and effortlessly picking her up off the ground. Her feet dangled in the air as she let out a loud squeal.

"I would use all my strength to swing underneath and then push them off using my legs. Then I can attack!" Lana said, still kicking into the air to no avail. Fortunately for her, her feet got tangled up with Adam's legs, knocking him off balance.

They fell right on top of each other; their faces inches away from one another. He smiled nervously as Lana slid over to sit flat on her butt beside him. Clearing his throat, he attempted to apologize.

"I-uh-that wasn't how I meant for that to happen. I'm sorry."

"It's fine, trust me. Don't even worry," Lana laughed, "Not bad for a weakling, huh? You should have stood your ground."

"Actually, you're kind of like a rag doll now that you mention it," Adam teased with signs of relief now visible on his face.

"Whoa! I didn't say I was a rag doll. I should have punched you in the throat; I could break your windpipes with ease!" Lana threatened, with a grin on her face.

"Now I regret teaching you that technique. I like my windpipes," Adam replied as they stood up. "One more thing left for us to do: I want to polish your punches and kicks." He directed Lana toward the punching bags across the room.

After they had finished, Lana's hands were numb and she was incapable of hitting anyone or anything.

"Right now, I really appreciate my guns, and I will never drop or ever forget mine," she said, rubbing her hands as they walked back to meet the others.

"It's not that bad, you actually did pretty well," Adam said with encouragement.

Instead of pitying herself, Lana switched subjects and talked about Adam's computers, "I have never seen such an amazing computer system. How did you hack into the Government system without them even realizing?"

"Oh, something my mother taught me. I'll be happy to show you sometime."

"Yes, please. To be honest, it's partly my fault Isabel is missing, I wasn't careful enough when I was trying to figure out the device."

"That device is above par. Don't blame yourself for anything. It took me days to even figure out that it was capable of lodging itself within the human body," Adam said. To save his ego, Lana decided not to add that she had determined that after a few hours of examination.

"Finding the logo inside the chip was the hardest for me, and the fact that I still have no idea what it does perplexes me," Lana said, hoping Adam would keep his guard down and tell her more of what he knew.

They saw Cory and Destiny conversing from a distance.

"What's your major?" Adam asked, impressed with the conversation he was having with Lana.

"Engineering. Well, it was before all the schools closed down," she replied nonchalantly. "So what else do you know about the device that I don't?"

"Not much, but I'll share what I know with you later, maybe we could even work together," Adam suggested, who seemed shocked a girl like Lana was studying engineering.

"Definitely! I want to get my hands on that computer of yours," Lana replied.

"My computer is my girlfriend. I'm not sure she will be okay with someone else touching her," Adam joked with a wink.

"I hope you know how sad that sounds," Lana said, laughing.

"What's so funny?" Destiny asked as she moved next to Adam to allow Lana and Cory to be closer to one another.

"Adam and his life as a computer nerd," Lana said with a big grin, which quickly vanished as Cory glared at her.

"You guys ready to go?" Adam said.

"Yeah, I could use a shower," Cory said.

They walked to the parking lot and drove off in a black BMW.

"So guys, who did you have more fun with? Me or Destiny?" Adam asked, while glimpsing at the rear-view mirror.

"Destiny. Hands down," Cory smiled. "At least with her, I don't have to worry about cheating."

Destiny glanced back and smiled.

I don't trust this bitch, Lana sulked.

18

"Ah, welcome back!" Bienaimé called out as they entered the house. "Adam, Destiny, tell me how they did!"

"They're both great shooters," Destiny announced.

"Yes, and great in combat too," Adam added.

"Good, good. You guys go wash up. I'll have dinner ready in a bit, there are things we must discuss," Bienaimé concluded.

The four tired young people did as they were told and went upstairs to their rooms.

"Do you want to shower first?" Lana asked, opening the bedroom door.

"No, you can go," Cory replied as he entered the room.

"Cory? Are we ever going to talk?" Lana asked, annoyed.

Instead of answering, Cory took a seat on a small chair by the window.

"Okay, fine," Lana snapped, stomping over to her suitcase to fetch her clothes. *This is the longest day of my life*, she thought, now regretting having told Cory about Doug. A little while later, freshly showered and dressed, they joined the others at the dinner table.

"So what did you have to talk to us about?" Cory asked.

"I've met up with your friend, Mr. Doug, and retrieved the devices. They are now locked up and safe, and will stay like that until we figure out what to do with them. Also, he gave me some important information about the set-up of the place."

Bienaimé tapped his fists on the edge of the table, and continued, "The good news is that the research facility only has guards stationed on the outside. The inside is filled with scientists, so we have little to worry about regarding the interior - but don't drop your guard." Stretching out his hands and laying them palms down on each side of plate, he leaned slightly forward and added, "Now, the bad news is that Doug has never been allowed to go to the prison, so there's no information there."

Sitting back, he shook his head slightly as he dropped his hands into his lap. He said in a calm, even voice, "Furthermore, we only have twenty men. I'll suggest using a five men squad to capture Dr. Phils, and the rest for the prison, seeing as it's more heavily guarded. Five men should be more than enough to handle the research facility, but with only fifteen men, we could still be outnumbered ten to one inside the prison."

Bienaimé paused, his lips tightly pressed together, looking around the table at each of the young people, in turn. After making sure he had their full attention, he said, his voice rising in volume, "If we're going to do this, we need to be prepared. Right now, I need your brains. The meeting is tomorrow at seven, so you have until then to think of something that would even the odds, because these people will not agree to fight if it's a suicide mission."

All of them nodded, deep in thought. They all had something worth fighting for. And the time for action was at long last coming.

"Oh, and one more thing," Bienaimé added, "Doug is scheduled to do a drop off exactly four days from now - so we will attack then. I have decided that you four will be part of the fifteen men assigned to the prison. You all have people you love in there, and I won't deny your reunion. I will lead the other group."

Picking up his fork, he waved it in Destiny and Adam's direction, "You two will tell Cory and Lana everything about the prison and facility. Cory, tomorrow I will check your house to see if they've tried to contact you. That is all for now. So eat up and enjoy - and remember, I need ideas from all of you intellectuals come tomorrow."

Cory finished his dinner, barely tasting the food. He wanted to be alone with his thoughts - but first, he needed to talk to Destiny and Adam. After dinner, the four went down to the secret basement to talk.

Adam pulled up the blueprints of both facilities on his computer screens.

"The buildings are secluded - about ten miles away from the nearest gas station - an ideal hide out. Lucky for us, there is nothing but trees around it, making for a perfect cover and vantage point. The research facility and prison are about two miles apart, and isolated from each other, and, from what we can tell, they also function separately from one another - but that's not to say they do not communicate with one another," Adam explained.

Stabbing his finger at the screen, he continued, "The research facility has two guards guarding each of the two towers, here, and there. And there are men stationed throughout the building. A barbed-wire fence encloses the entire area, and there's another guard who does security-checks of everyone entering and exiting the building. I rank the security at the research facility a medium at best."

Taking a deep breath and scratching his chin, he said, "The real problem is with the prison. It's your standard maximum-security prison. The area is surrounded by a double 30-foot razor fence, and there are observation towers at every corner—"

"Not to mention the armed patrol vehicles, motion sensor, and the whole nine yards," Destiny added.

"Going at them head on is a bad idea. We need to attack them from the inside," Cory suggested.

"Let's hope we can figure out how to get in," Adam said, pushing his chair away from the computer and standing. "I've downloaded all the information on this USB key for you and Lana. The layout of the prison is on there, but keep in mind it's from a few years back. They might've made modifications to the place. If you guys can go through it more thoroughly, we can meet up again, say three p.m., to discuss what our plan will be."

"Sounds good, and remember guys, we need to find a way in first, before we start a gunfight," Destiny added.

Cory and Lana nodded as they journeyed back to their room, leaving Destiny and Adam in the basement to talk. Lana was eager to do her own research, but she faced one problem. Adam had given the USB key to Cory, and she felt awkward asking for it. But she had been looking for a reason to talk to Cory, and now she had one.

"Cory, can I use the USB key? I just want to copy the files onto my computer," she said, hoping to strike up a conversation.

Cory replied by throwing the USB key toward Lana without looking - definitely not the response she was hoping for. Stretching out her arms, she caught the key from his careless throw. Lana was sure she would not be able to concentrate in their room with the never-ending awkwardness between the two. Picking up her things, she ventured out, looking for a place to come up with her own plan. The task proved troublesome,

Bienaimé's house had so many rooms and artifacts that Lana kept getting distracted trying to find somewhere to work in.

At last, she stumbled upon a room with an overview of the backyard. The view was perfect. It overlooked Bienaimé's tennis and basketball courts, pool and garden. Sitting next to the window, she began her research. Opening the files on the USB, she read them one by one. Lana wanted to make sure she knew the blueprint of the facility, and in particular, the prison, as if she had been there a thousand times. Finally, unable to concentrate any longer from sheer exhaustion, she took a break to admire the backyard.

I wonder if this is the kind of view Grandma has. Can't believe I haven't seen her new place yet. I bet it's just as nice as this one. Without thinking, Lana reached for her phone and called her grandmother.

"Hello, darling!" Lana's grandmother answered, with obvious excitement.

"Wow, Grandma, you sound so excited."

"I haven't heard from my grandchild in a very long time. I miss her voice."

"Sorry, there's a lot going on here," Lana said, ashamed that she'd neglected her grandmother this way.

"Well then, fill me in," the older woman insisted.

"I'm not in the mood to do a lot of filling in… Hey, do you think I can come stay with you when I'm done with everything here?" Lana said with melancholy in her voice.

"You're always welcome here, you know that. But you've always turned down my invitations. What's happened with you and Cory?" her grandmother asked, having picked up, as always, on her granddaughter's behavior and temperament.

"I'd rather not talk about it, Grandma. Can't we talk about the weather or something else, please?"

"No young lady, you tell me what's going on right now. You sound defeated. What's wrong? What happened?" Lana's grandmother's tone shifted from being nonchalant to a fierce lioness, ready to protect her cub.

After a few seconds of hesitation and looking up at the ceiling and trying not to cry, Lana broke down. Her voice cracked as she spoke, "I made a stupid mistake, and I admitted it to Cory, and now he hates me."

She couldn't compose herself. She wished for nothing more than to lay her head on her grandmother's lap and cry until her tears ran out.

"What did you do? Take a deep breath, then go over the events clearly, darling," Her grandmother said gently, wanting to hear all the details before giving advice.

"Okay, so Cory and I always fought. It was so hostile all the time. If it wasn't one thing, it was another. I couldn't remember the last time I had genuinely enjoyed myself." Lana stopped, sniffed, and then dabbed her eyes before continuing. "So when I was having fun with Doug, I got carried away and ended up kissing him. After I realized what I had done, I told him to stop and pushed him off me. Then Cory came…"

Lana continued telling her grandmother a G-rated version of the events that followed between Cory and her. Bowing her head to her chest, she blurted out, all in one breath, "I told Cory, and now he's so upset with me. He completely ignores me and only talks to me to order me to do things or to make jabs at me. I'm trying to show him that I'm sorry, but it isn't getting any easier. At this point, I just want to curl up in a ball and cry my eyes out."

"Slow down, Lana. Take a breather," her grandmother coaxed, just like she used to when Lana was littler. "Honey, you may not have noticed, but you're already crying your eyes out," she joked, attempting to lighten the mood. "Look, the relationship you have with Cory is complicated and the two of you have been forced to mature quickly - especially that boy."

Lana's grandmother launched into her analysis of the situation, "But you're not in the wrong for being vulnerable, which, knowing you, is completely expected behavior. How long did you think hostility, and arguments would go on before they took a toll on your psyche? In my opinion, Cory isn't completely a man yet; he has so much difficulty expressing his emotions. This is not a good thing - he's flawed, like every other human being. What makes him less of a person is that he refuses to address his shortcomings. Ignoring you isn't a positive way of addressing his hurt from what you did with Doug - and trust me, honey, he's hurt…extremely."

"I know, Grandma, but he's not going to listen to anything I say. I'm at my breaking point. After all I've dealt with, and all the things I've stayed for. I could endure it all because I knew he didn't mean it; it was his anger and hysteria talking and not him. But when he's calm and cold, it seems like he actually hates me, and it hurts so much more this way," Lana admitted.

"Darling, I have no idea how Cory will respond, but you need to tell him what you just told me. I will make travel arrangements for you anyway. How does two weeks sound? You should be ready by then."

"Sounds good. Thanks, Grandma," Lana said, still sobbing.

"Lana, darling, stop crying now. You don't want puffy red eyes. I think you've cried enough for today. Promise me that you'll tell Cory, and that you'll be strong for your last few days."

Lana promised, although she wasn't sure she could speak with Cory the way her grandmother expected her to. Maybe it was for the best to leave everything behind and go be with her grandmother. She hadn't realized how much she had missed her. But for now, she had to put her emotions aside and focus on the mission at hand. She'd promised herself that she would rescue Isabel, and she wouldn't break that promise.

19

When Lana awoke the next morning, Cory was up doing research on his laptop.

"...find anything yet?" she asked, still yawning.

Again, Cory failed to acknowledge her, and his eyes never strayed from his computer screen.

Lana scowled at Cory as she made her way into the bathroom. *Ugh! I can't take this anymore; I need to talk to him... I'm going to talk to him right now. But is it too soon? No, it must be done now,* Lana pondered, washing her face and brushing her teeth.

"Be strong, Lana, you can do this. Look at him straight in the eyes and don't take no for an answer... and don't cry," Lana prepped herself before walking back into the bedroom.

She took a deep breath before marching up to Cory, who was sitting in his chair, and with a stern voice, she said, "Cory, we need to talk."

Cory paused for a moment; flabbergasted at the confidence Lana had mustered to approach him. *She must be crazy;* he thought, sucking his teeth.

"Lana... get out of my face," he snarled.

"N-no!" Lana stuttered, struggling to keep her composure. "I'm not going anywhere until we talk this through."

Glaring into Lana's eyes, he saw she was serious, and getting rid of her would not be as easy as just telling her to. Closing his laptop, he gazed at her.

"Lana, please I don't have time for this, and there's nothing to talk about," he said, trying to convince her to leave him alone.

Don't take no for an answer, Lana's conscience reminded her. She stood in front of him, folded her arms together, and shook her head no.

"Okay, if you want to talk, then talk. I'm listening. Let's put everything out on the table, but let this be the last time," Cory lashed out.

"Fine, I plan on saying everything I have to say anyways," Lana replied.

It was the face off before the match, and the tension in the air was thickening. This conversation would only brew another fight, but it was too late to stop it. As much as Cory wanted to be left alone, sooner or later they had to talk. A few seconds went by with complete silence. Lana was thinking of how to present her argument, while Cory beckoned her with hand gestures, urging her to speak. She took a deep breath and began.

"Okay, I've hurt you. And there's no excuse for what I did, and you have every reason to hate me - because I hate myself for it too. I hope you'll forgive me or at least understand why I did what I did."

Cory didn't bother looking at Lana while she spoke. Instead, he kept his head down and listened to every word she said, searching for a flaw in her story.

"It's just that we've been fighting everyday nonstop," Lana continued, struggling to keep her voice calm and even. "And I wasn't in a good state of mind because of it. You didn't really make me feel wanted - and, after a year, it was like I was wasting your air. I tried so hard to get you to open up to me, but it never worked.

"I didn't know what I was to you, and even now, I'm still not sure what I am to you. I wasn't sure if you even cared for me anymore, or if you still wanted this - us. When you left me with Doug, I was so vulnerable, and then you forgot to call me about Isabel, as if I wouldn't be worried half to death. It didn't seem like you cared for me. Then Doug opened up to me and told me stories—the way you used too."

Now that she had started talking, the words flow smoother. She dropped her arms to her side, taking a deep breath, she continue, "He reminded me so much of how you used to be, that I naturally gravitated toward him. He appreciated me being there, and then one thing led to another, we kissed...and that was it. Trust me when I say we did nothing else but kiss. It was stupid, and I don't like him at all. I was just missing you...the old you."

Cory lifted his head up to look into Lana's eyes and grasp her soul.

"I'm not sure what to believe anymore," he said. "The way I see it, you crossed the line when you kissed Doug. You betrayed my trust, and now you expect me to believe that you guys did nothing but kiss—"

"But that's all we did. I swear!" Lana interrupted.

"I don't believe you, and that's not even the most fucked-up thing about it," Cory said, through gritted teeth.

"Okay, what then?"

"I'll get to that. First off, I admit I should have called you right away and told you about Bell, but I was trying to calm her down and figure out what was going on. Regardless, I still planned on calling you afterwards. The fact that you beat me to it is unfortunate - that's my bad - but do you really think so badly of me to say that I don't care about you?"

Cory lowered his eyes and added, "Everything I do is because of you! Not a single decision is made without you in mind. Why is it I'm always so protective of you if you don't think I care?"

"I don't know," Lana murmured, shrugging her shoulders.

Looking back into her eyes, he said, "Why is it that every guy who looks at you funny always puts me on edge?" Cory clinched his fists as he continued, "Time and time again I have shown you that I care, but nah, you don't want the actions - you want the words. I have always shown you that I cared the best way I knew how, but that's never been good enough for you - and I always took the blame whenever something went wrong in our relationship, but now that you've kissed somebody else, you still want to stand here and blame me, Lana?"

Lana stood still, letting every word resonate through her. The mixture of the guilt and the hurt in Cory's eyes were too much to bear. She tried to control her emotions, but stinging tears lingered on the edges of her eye, waiting to slide down her crimson face.

"Stop acting like you're never in the wrong and man up to the choices you make. You kissing Doug - that's not what makes me sick, though - it's the fact that you have absolutely zero respect for me that gets me. How dare you kiss that bitch, and then have sex with me on the same night? How dare you kiss him and then kiss me right after, you didn't even brush your teeth yet! How could you ever disrespect me like that with a man who doesn't even care for you," Cory said with moist eyes.

"But—" Lana started only to get interrupted.

"But nothing, Lana," Cory exclaimed, slamming his fist on his lap. "You can chalk it up however you want; it still doesn't change a thing. I have more respect for myself to ever let you put me in the same league as

Doug."

"You're not," Lana shouted. "I'm so, so sorry, Cory. Please - you've got to believe me! I know how much you care for me. If I could take it back, I would, but I can't. Doug means nothing to me; I love you!"

"I see that you're sorry, but I can't think of 'us' right now. Lana, I need to get my family back, and I need you in order to do that. And if I go into that prison and never come back, I want you to know…" Cory took a calming breath, "I want you to know that I love you, and nothing will ever change that. But as far as us, right now, Lana, I don't know…"

Lana shook her head, numb at hearing Cory say, "I love you." But these were not the circumstances she envisioned hearing those precious words from him. She stood there crying. She couldn't bear the thought of losing Cory and feared that it was happening.

Cory stood to console her. As he hugged Lana, he said, "Stop crying, I will always do what's best for you. I need time to figure us out, but right now my sister needs the both of us. I need you to be strong - for me. Can you do that?"

She nodded as she pressed her head onto Cory's chest, drenching his shirt with tears.

They stood in each other's arms for several minutes until Lana pulled away and excused herself into the bathroom. She'd needed that conversation with Cory, and she still had hope that she could win back his trust and their relationship. When she walked out of the bathroom, she saw Cory had not moved from his chair.

He looked at her and kindly said, "Hey, can you help me out with these blueprints?"

Lana nodded and smiled, "Yeah, sure."

They went over the blueprint until it was time to meet with the others. They all gathered around the dining room table to discuss their plans over lunch.

"Okay, so what do we have so far?" Adam said.

"Well, the first thing we should do is destroy their communication. That way, when we hit them, they'll be running around like their heads were cut off," Cory replied.

"I should be able to scramble their radio signals," Adam said.

"Great, but how about the security cameras?" Destiny asked.

"Lana might be able to access their cameras, giving us direct feed while sabotaging theirs," Cory responded.

"Yup, you just have to show me how to hack into the government database without being caught. That way I can use the same method on the security camera," Lana said, looking at Adam.

"Sounds good, but the cameras might not be online –you might have to get close enough to the control center to hack into it," Adam said.

"We'll manage. Now, I don't think we should split up. Instead, let's station two or three people to keep an eye on the prison while the rest will be at the research facility. We'll capture Dr. Phils and use him to gain access to the prison. With the added men, it'll be a lot easier to take control," Cory suggested.

"Once we're inside, we need to take control of the armory. That way, we can cut their firepower in half. We should do that right after we take over the control center," Destiny added.

"Good idea! Lana, Adam, you two must remain safe at all times. This will not work without you two being able to access their systems," Cory said.

They continued to discuss and tweak their plan until they were confident enough to propose it to Bienaimé.

"Good work guys," Adam said as they got up. "I'll tell Professor we came up with the perfect plan."

They scattered into different parts of the house. Instead of going back to the bedroom with Lana, Cory headed to the game room. He was busy playing pool when Destiny appeared.

"Oh, hey! Wassup, Destiny?" Cory greeted.

"Nothing much. I came up here to relax," she replied.

"Oh yeah? Well, I'm just about done here if you need your space."

"No, stay…I could use the company, and maybe I can teach you a thing or two about pool," Destiny said with a smile.

The two spent a couple of hours talking over a game of pool. Cory felt comfortable around Destiny. He wasn't pressured to express himself, like he did with Lana, and his thoughts and words flowed freely.

"Thanks for taking us in. I really appreciate how you guys have treated us," Cory said, grabbing his pool stick and lowering his body over the table.

"Oh, no problem! It's nice having company for a change," Destiny replied, watching Cory take aim. "You sure about that shot?"

"Yup," Cory said, not breaking concentration.

"I don't know," Destiny drawled. "Maybe you need me to show you how to hold that stick."

"Nope," Cory said, hitting a stripped ball into the corner pocket. "See, it's all about the stroke."

Destiny laughed, "Lucky shot."

"I smell jealousy on your breath," Cory teased, nudging Destiny on her arm. "Hey, I've been meaning to ask you - who is it that the Government took away from you?"

"Her name is Kelly. She's my best friend. Well, we're practically sisters," Destiny replied, rubbing chalk on the tip of her pool stick. "We did everything together. Funny, she even waited a year for me to graduate just so we could attend college together." She paused, tilting her head down. "At the hardest point of my life, when suicide seemed like the only option, she was the one there for me – the only one who understood. If it wasn't for her support, I don't know if I'd even be here today... Man, I can't wait to see her again."

"Don't worry, we'll get her back...all of them," Cory said, placing his hand on her shoulder. "How about Adam, who did he lose?"

"His fiancé or girlfriend. I'm not too sure, which is which. He never talks about her that much," Destiny answered.

They played a few more games until Lana walked in on them. She wore a blank expression, but forged a fake smile when Cory and Destiny noticed her.

"Hey Lana, come join us!" Destiny said with enthusiasm.

"No, it's fine. I'm looking for the USB that Adam gave us. I might have left it here last night," Lana lied.

Before things got awkward, she pretended to look around for the USB before making her exit. She had wondered where Cory was since he'd been gone for so long. She never expected to find him hanging out with Destiny. Pacing back to the bedroom, she grabbed her headphones. *I don't trust her*, she sulked, as she lay in bed, letting the music take her mind off Cory.

*

When Cory walked in, Lana was staring at the ceiling with music blaring from her headphones. She felt his presence, but ignored it.

"Lana, Lana, Lana," Cory shouted to be heard.

"What?" Lana said, taking off her headset.

What's gotten into her? Cory did not appreciate Lana's sudden attitude.

"Bienaimé just got home. We're going to go talk to him now," he said, choosing not to acknowledge her current mood.

Lana said nothing in reply. Wordlessly, she followed Cory downstairs, where they all shared the details of their plan with Bienaimé.

"That might actually work," Bienaimé said, climbing up the stairs. "Now, let me get out of these dirty clothes, then we can head over to the meeting spot."

A while later, Bienaimé came back down dressed in an Italian suit topped by a farmer's hat.

"All right, let's go," he said as he guided them to the garage. "Adam, you guys take Cory and Lana in your car. I'll drive solo."

Cory and Lana sat quietly in the back as Adam followed Bienaimé off the premises. They drove to a secluded area, not far away, in a small town that appeared to be deserted. It was six in the evening, and no one was in sight. Adam pulled up into an abandoned old warehouse behind Bienaimé. They exited the vehicles and walked to the building. As soon as they opened the door, they were stopped in their tracks - two men dressed in black appeared, carrying semi-automatic weapons and ready to attack.

"Easy, son, it's me," Bienaimé said, prompting them to lower their guns.

"Sorry, sir. Go ahead," they replied in unison, stepping aside to let them pass.

The warehouse was empty except for a few wooden crates scattered here and there, and the eye-stinging odor of rats and rusty nails permeated everything. The windows were boarded up, making it dark and gloomy. Cory and Lana moved cautiously. The place looked like it might collapse.

A few other people roamed about, but no one acknowledged them. Bienaimé led them to a set of rotten wooden doors. Before entering, he faced Cory and the others.

"Past this point, I'm only allowed to have two personnel with me, so which one of y'all is brave enough?" Bienaimé asked.

"Let Cory go - he probably knows the plan better than any of us," Adam suggested.

"Okay, I'll take Cory and Destiny. Adam, you stay here and watch over Lana...we should be back shortly," Bienaimé ordered.

Everyone nodded, except Lana. She wasn't thrilled with Destiny escorting Cory. Sick with jealousy, she stayed back and watched as Cory, Destiny, and Bienaimé disappeared behind the doors.

The door creaked closed behind them as they stepped inside. Cory was at once overwhelmed by the powerful stench of mildew and mold. He covered his mouth and nose, but it did little to filter out the smell. They kept walking until they stopped in front of a locked door. Bienaimé knocked twice and waited for an answer.

A man opened the door, and just like the other guards; he was dressed in black and carried a semi-automatic weapon. He glanced briefly at Bienaimé before letting him in. The room was dark, the only light coming from an overhead lamp dangling over a huge round table. Four men sat around the table, with two others standing to their side.

"Charles, Jeff, Alex, Zaire," Bienaimé said, walking to his seat.

"Ah, nice of you to finally show," one of the men said to Bienaimé as he took his seat at the table.

"Nice to see you too, Jeff," Bienaimé smiled.

Jeff was a middle-aged Arabian man with an evenly tanned skin and a silky, well-groomed beard hiding his charming smile. Compared to the others, he dressed in a casual style, wearing dark-blue jeans and a white shirt. He was tall and thin. His face was both intimidating and welcoming at the same time. With just the tilt of his head, he could easily go from a predator to the hero.

Cory and Destiny took their positions standing beside Bienaimé and waited for the meeting to commence.

"Jeff, I heard you have some news for us," Bienaimé said.

"Yes, I assigned a couple of my men to search for fresh water supplies that we could use instead of relying on the government. Unfortunately, the government is heavily guarding every single water supply out there," Jeff replied.

"That's not news. We already know that. Besides, most of those waters are contaminated anyway. It's being guarded so people won't drink the water in the first place, or so they say," Charles interrupted Jeff.

"Let me finish. Well, it turns out the water isn't contaminated. We got a sample and after some tests, nothing out of the ordinary came up." Jeff started tapping his finger on the table. "The scientific reports that the government published, and the people badly sick in the news after drinking the water, are all bogus. They did it merely to have an excuse to own the most powerful natural resource in the world." He stopped tapping to stroke his beard. "After finding that out, I deployed half my team to investigate the food industry. I'm thinking the food isn't contaminated either…They've got us starving out here for nothing - but we will soon find out."

Bienaimé laughed hysterically, "I paid them one million dollars to have running water for the year. I should have known they wouldn't be dumb enough to contaminate the world's water supplies. But, you've got to hand it to them; they sold it good."

"Yeah, but there's little we can do with that information. Not right now, not without public backing. We can't just come out and say to the public 'Oh look, the government lied and is keeping the water from you,' they won't believe us. They won't fight with us," Zaire added.

Zaire was a sight to behold, with mysterious features, being both African and Colombian. Although his appearance was African, his mannerisms and dialect said differently. His accent was pronounced, and it was easy to decipher that Spanish was his language of choice. He was dark-skinned like cocoa, but his eyes were as green as emeralds.

"Well, I got somebody who they will have to listen to," Bienaimé said.

"Who?" they all asked.

"I've gathered some intel, and I am certain I know where they are keeping the missing people in my district. If we free them, they will run back home and tell their loved ones exactly who did this to them. It'll be the start of a revolution, and we will grow in numbers and in strength," Bienaimé responded.

"Is this why you brought us here?" Zaire asked, intrigued.

"Yes, it is," Bienaimé said.

"Okay, I'm assuming you have a plan then," he replied.

"Yes, I do, but I will need all your help. We're going to capture Dr. Damian Phils in the process."

"Dr. Damian Phils? You know we can't get close enough to touch that man," Charles shouted.

"Yes, before we didn't know his schedule or how armed the people around him were, but that was before. My new colleague over here has provided me with an informant who can get as close to him as we are to one another right now," Bienaimé said, pointing to Cory.

"Okay, now I'm listening. What's the plan?" Zaire asked.

"The missing people are being held in an old prison with a research facility a couple miles away. We will move as a unit and take control of that research facility, capturing Dr. Phils with it. Then, we will gather intel before moving on to the prison and taking control of it from the inside out," Bienaimé informed.

"Do you know what we're dealing with?" Charles asked.

"The research facility won't be too complicated - the prison is where we're going to need all the manpower we have. We're outnumbered ten to one, but once we free the captives, the numbers will be in our favor," Bienaimé answered.

They all sat and listened to what Bienaimé had to say. After Bienaimé spoke, the room went silent. It was their turn to talk and answer the important question of whether they would support Bienaimé in his quest.

"I'm in," Zaire announced, breaking the silence.

"Me too," Charles and Jeff both said right after.

"Yes, you can count me in as well," Alex concluded.

Alex was Charles's twin brother. They looked almost identical except for the hair. While Charles kept his hair short, Alex had long brown hair, which had been slicked back into a low bun. Alex had a self-assured demeanor that Charles couldn't mimic. Everything about him portrayed the look of a boss. From his gold hoop earring that glistened every time light touched it, to his gold watch that cost as much as Cory's house.

Cory was thrilled all were on board with the plan. There were three days left before Doug made his shipment, and everything was falling in place. It was the first time Cory felt like he was doing something right. Everything about this moment seemed destined.

Shaking hands as the assembly broke up, they promised to meet for the debriefing after the mission. Cory was given the responsibility of providing each of them with an electronic copy of the plan.

Bienaimé was smiling from ear to ear as they approached Adam and Lana.

"This, my friends, is the start of a revolution. And when justice is done, it is a joy to the righteous, but a source of terror to evildoers," he said, strutting back to his car.

20

The next day was like any other. Cory and Lana got up and resumed their training while Bienaimé headed out into the street wearing his rugged clothing. With only two days left before implementing their plan, everyone was on edge. Tension between Cory and Lana had calmed down, except when Cory would bring up Destiny's name in a conversation.

Everyone did their best to relax. Cory hung out with Destiny in the game room, leaving Lana in the bedroom. Instead of moping around, Lana kept herself busy familiarizing herself with the hacking technique Adam had taught her. When loneliness built to an unbearable level, she called her grandmother.

She knew Cory's wounds were still too raw, and they were both still emotional about the 'Doug situation'. Cory had resorted to leaving her alone in their room. It was the only way he knew to ease the tension between them. The only time they talked was right before they went to bed. Although Lana slept right next to him, they could have been miles apart.

When Cory returned to the room, Lana was sitting on the edge of the bed, typing on her computer.

"Hey, what are you doing?" he asked as he walked in.

"Just looking at the designs of the security camera," Lana responded.

"Oh, okay. Well, dinner should be ready soon. I'm going to hop in the shower," Cory said, grabbing his towel and heading into the bathroom.

"Okay."

Their conversation, like many of their recent ones, was short and simple, leaving no room for disputes.

*

"This looks great, Bienaimé!" Lana said as they sat down at the dining room table.

"Thank you, I dipped the steak in my special sauce," he replied.

Cory couldn't remember the last time he'd had steak, and he couldn't wait to sink his teeth into it. In that exact moment, he needed to thank Bienaimé for all he had done for them.

"No, thank you, Bienaimé," Cory said. "With everything that's been going on, I didn't get a chance to say thank you. Thanks for the place to stay, water, food, and your support. Destiny, Adam, thank you too, for making us feel so at home."

"Save the fireworks, son, there's no need for thanks. I'm just grateful you chose to fight for our cause. And I believe I speak for the others as well, when I say it's a pleasure having you guys stay with us," Bienaimé said as Destiny and Adam nodded. "-But before I get lost in all this delicious food, I've got news for you.

"There was a letter left on your porch. It wasn't marked or signed - it just had a phone number on it and a message that read, 'If you want her back.' Looks like they're done with Isabel and are waiting for you to act. But little do they know that we will strike them where it hurts."

"I can hardly wait," Cory replied.

Lana reached over and put her hand over Cory's, and squeezed it.

"Good! Over the next couple of days, I need you guys to try to relax. Enjoy yourselves; enjoy each other. Because when it comes down to it, I hope you guys don't hold back. It will be a war zone out there, and you can't hesitate. You're going up against people you don't even know - some good and some bad. When you're out there, you've got to have each other's backs and act quickly. And when it's all said and done, know that you did what you had to."

Everyone nodded as Bienaimé continued, "Destiny, Lana - don't torment yourselves for the actions you take out there; there is a difference between murder and killing. When you murder someone, it's premeditated and driven by malice. But when you kill someone, it's either accidental or for self-preservation. With that being said, remember that they can't die, so when you shoot, aim for their heads and knock them out."

Even though Bienaimé's words were unsettling, his manner commanded their undivided attention. He was a man filled with wisdom, and the tone and tenor of his voice brought calmness to a stressful subject.

When he finished speaking, he looked around the table, catching each person's eyes with his. "Eat up, kids. I can't wait to see the look on your faces when you taste this steak."

For a moment, Bienaimé beamed as he watched them take bites of his speciality dish. Then he too sliced off a piece, and savored it.

"Mm hmm. This sure is good," he said, rolling his eyes.

Laughter resounded throughout the open space, and everyone ate heartily, forgetting for a few minutes what was coming soon.

As the meal came to a close, Cory was again on edge. He was ringing with excitement, knowing he would be reunited with his mother and sister — in just a matter of days.

Suspense and anxiety settled over Lana as she finished eating. Of course, she was excited to get Isabel and Cory's mother back, but she dreaded telling Cory she would be leaving him right after the mission. She pushed aside her tormented thoughts, as best she could, focusing instead on the amazing plan they had developed, and how she couldn't wait to see it unfold.

*

The next day was the calm before the storm of the revolution- the last day before the rescue mission. The house remained silent throughout the day; everyone moved around barely speaking - even Bienaimé was quiet. After dinner, they retired early, wanting to be well-rested for the day ahead.

*

Cory woke up earlier than usual. *Today is the day*, he thought as he went into the bathroom to freshen up. When he came out, Lana was awake, playing with her phone.

"Morning," Cory greeted.

"Good morning," Lana responded, walking to the bathroom. It was her turn to shower and get ready. When she was done, they joined the others to review their plans.

"Destiny, Adam - go check in with the others while I'll take Cory and Lana to go see Doug," Bienaimé instructed.

After eating, Destiny and Adam went to the basement to call Charles, Alex, Zaire, and Jeff. Meanwhile, Cory and Lana hopped in the car with Bienaimé and drove to Doug's house. He was already outside, waiting for them.

"Right on time," Doug called out as they pulled up into the driveway.

"Today's the big day. I trust that everything is on schedule," Bienaimé said as he stepped out the car.

"Yup! The truck is set to be delivered at nine this evening, and I also made sure that it won't be targeted by any raiders," Doug replied.

"Perfect, take this," Bienaimé said as he handed Doug a bracelet. "Make sure you wear it at all times, in case we lose you."

"Yeah, you just make sure I'm in the clear; I don't want any of this being traced back to me," Doug said.

"Don't worry, just do what you were instructed to, and everything will be fine," Bienaimé replied as he climbed back into the driver's seat and drove off. Cory and Lana hadn't bothered to get out of the car during Bienaimé's exchange with Doug, and he took notice.

"Is everything all right?" Bienaimé asked. "I thought you guys would want to see your friend."

"Yeah, everything is cool. And he's no friend of mine," Cory said, while Lana remained silent in the seat next to him.

Bienaimé laughed and continued his drive back home. When they arrived, Destiny and Adam were sitting in the living room, watching television.

"Any news?" Bienaimé called out.

"Everything is good to go. We're set to meet up with the others at six for a briefing, and then we have an hour to get everyone ready and positioned," Destiny replied.

"Great. Everyone should be ready to go no later than four-thirty," Bienaimé declared, marching up the stairs.

21

The alarm went off - Lana woke, snuggled up to Cory. She pulled back to her side of the bed before checking the time. *It's three thirty.* As she got up, she looked back at Cory still sound asleep. He looked so peaceful, void of earthly troubles. It would be shameful to wake him, but it was time to get ready.

"Cory, wake up. It's time," she said, shaking his shoulders.

"What time is it?" Cory yawned, stretching out his arms.

"Almost four."

Now awake, Cory took a moment to gather his thoughts while Lana waited for him to spring into action.

"All right, let's get dressed," he said, jumping to his feet and moving toward the closet.

He pulled out all black clothing, prompting Lana to do the same. She prayed this would be the last time she had to wear that dreadful ensemble; nothing ever followed donning this outfit except for bloodshed. After smoothing down the black crewneck, and strapping her holster to the upper thigh of her black cargo pants, she walked over to Cory, who was dressed in the same attire. He had placed a pair of bulletproof vests, along with both of their gun cases, on the bed.

Lana could sense how tense Cory was just by looking into his eyes, and if that hadn't given him away, his twitching hands did. His demeanor changed; the time for games was over. Opening their gun cases, they checked their weapons thoroughly. They each slid a loaded magazine into their handguns before securing them in their holsters. After stuffing several more filled magazines into their pockets, and just as Lana reached for her vest, Cory's hands pulled her to him. He kissed her forehead and whispered, "I love you."

Tears rolled down Lana's cheeks as Cory spoke those precious words. It was his first and only act of affection since she told him the truth. But that didn't matter - it was everything she could have asked for. They stood there for a moment in each other's arms before Lana pushed away and continued to get ready. Again, she felt his hands on her.

But this time, Cory took Lana's vest, pulling it over her head before slowly lowering it, letting the front-panel rest on her curvaceous chest and the back-panel on the small of her back. Reaching down for her waist strap, he pulled it tight, tugging on the bottom of the panels to ensure that the Velcro was gripped securely.

"Is that comfortable enough?" he asked.

"Y-yeah, that's fine," Lana stuttered, trying not to blush.

Cory grabbed his own vest and pulled it over his head. Before he got the chance to adjust his waist strap, he felt Lana's soft hands pulling it tight from behind.

"Thanks," he said, looking back.

This would be the perfect time for Lana to say something - anything at all - to Cory. She could have told him how she planned to go to her grandmother's house after they'd finished their mission - but before she could speak, there was a knock on the door.

"Come in," Cory yelled.

The door opened, and Destiny and Adam stepped in.

"Hey, are you guys ready?" Destiny asked.

"Yup!" Lana replied, snatching her sniper rifle and pulling the strap over her shoulders, letting the weapon hang on her side. Cory grabbed his M16 and followed the others downstairs.

"Hey, do you guys mind if I borrow a side arm for my sister?" Cory asked.

"Help yourself to whatever you like in the basement," Adam replied.

Cory hurried to the basement while the others waited for him near the garage door. Bienaimé was already in his car with the engine on. As soon as Cory returned, they exited the house and hopped into Adam's BMW.

"You folks ready to go?" A loud voice came screeching through a radio that was in the middle of the dashboard.

Grabbing the walkie-talkie, Destiny said, "Yes Uncle, lead the way."

They drove back to the abandoned warehouse. The same two hostile doormen, dressed in black and holding semi-automatic weapons, greeted them. At least twenty people scattered around inside. Bienaimé excused himself once he spotted Jeff, Alex, Charles and Zaire conversing in a corner.

Destiny and Adam introduced Cory and Lana to as many people as they could. Cory was surprised how diverse the group was. They came from all walks of life - some were Europeans, while others were from Africa or Asia. Everyone was ready for war, but you wouldn't be able to tell from the conversations circulating. It was a room full of laughter. No-one sounded serious, but their mood changed upon being summoned. It was a quarter to six when Zaire gathered everyone together for the briefing.

"I want to thank everyone here. Today is the day where we will take back a piece of our lives and let them know that those who still believe in true freedom are more than willing to fight! Now, without further ado, I will let Professor Bienaimé take the floor," Zaire said.

Bienaimé emerged to face the crowd, then stood in silence for a moment. He made sure every set of ears and eyes were focused on him.

"I would also like to thank everyone for being here," Bienaimé started. "As some of you are aware, today we're going to free those who have been held captive for over a year now." He raised his right hand; his fingers were stiffly spread and slightly bent. "We will also capture the infamous Dr. Phils himself. This operation is just the beginning. From here, we will free everyone who is being detained by our so-called 'government.' We're outnumbered ten to one, but we're fighting for the freedom of our loved ones, and we will not be defeated."

He balled his hand into a fist and started pacing back and forth. "When you're out there, remember what you're fighting for, and you will see that you will conquer your enemies, and they shall fall before you. Five of you can chase off a hundred, and a hundred of you can put ten thousand to flight - your enemies will fall before you."

Bienaimé stopped his pacing and with open palms, he extended his hands toward the crowd. "This, my brothers and sisters, is a promise -and when you're on that battlefield, feeling scared or stumbling, just look around this room; there are people in here that are ready to pick you up and fight your battle. We're all here for each other and our loved ones. Fight for the cause; fight for each other. I have high hopes for each one of you - I pray that you guys don't let me down."

There was a loud uproar, accompanied by guns pounding in the air. The atmosphere was electric - full of excitement and fight. Bienaimé waited for the crowd to settle down before he outlined the plan and dismissed them to get their things together.

"Be ready to move out in twenty," he yelled as everyone prepared.

Inspired by his speech, Lana wanted to show Bienaimé her appreciation. She sought to find the old man while he was still strolling around.

"Hey, Bienaimé," she said, tapping his shoulder.

"Oh, hey darling," Bienaimé replied, mildly surprised. "What can I do for you?"

"Oh, nothing. I just wanted to tell you that what you said was really inspiring," Lana confessed, blushing.

"Oh, darling, stop that. You inspire me."

"How?" Lana asked, shocked. She'd never expected to be an inspiration for anyone.

"The way you are with that boy. I can tell that things aren't going too well between you two right now, but you're still here fighting. You have everything to lose and nothing to gain but his happiness, and yet you still fight for him. The loyalty and the kindness that you show for him…it reminds me every day why I still fight. Have you ever heard of the saying 'a friend loves at all times, and a brother is born for adversity'?"

"No," Lana answered.

"Well, you see, a brother, or in your case a sister, will always show loyalty in times of calamity. That is not to say that they will only show loyalty in times of need; but in dire times, their natural instinct is to love and support their brother or sister. For example, if someone accused my brother of anything, I would deny it to my dying breath, and if it turned out the accusations held true…well, that's family business. The funny thing is, that kind of adversity is often the only thing that brings family together.

"Now a friend - a real friend - loves you at all times, even when it hurts them. They owe you no loyalty, but act like they do. Oftentimes, they are the ones who you run to when you want to complain about your family. They are the friends who stick closer to you than a brother. A person is lucky to have at least one of these people in their lives, and you, my darling, have blessed Cory with the best gift he could possibly have…you guys have blessed each other."

Bienaimé's words were comforting, and Lana was so overwhelmed with joy that tears rolled down her checks. He embraced her.

"Don't cry, darling, or you're gonna make me cry," he teased.

Lana laughed and hugged him tighter.

"Thanks, Bienaimé," she said.

"No problem," Bienaimé replied, "and Lana?"

"Yeah?"

"Whatever you did to that boy…fix it."

Lana laughed once more before going back to join the others. Everyone was making their way to their vehicles; it was almost time for them to take their positions. Bienaimé, Jeff, Alex, Zaire and Charles were the first ones to drive off the premises, while the others followed behind.

They parked at a nearby camping site. From there, it was a ten-minute march through the woods, stopping twenty yards from the wire fence surrounding the research facility. Hidden by bushes, they waited quietly in the comfort of the shadows. It was a quarter past seven, and there were still at least two hours left until Doug made his delivery.

Cory glanced up above. The tall trees blocked sunlight from reaching them. *It'll be pitch black soon - the only light coming from the building lights and the two tower lights rotating around.*

They had counted twenty-eight armed men stationed around the research facility, and the darkness was their biggest ally.

Still, as night came, time didn't move forward fast enough. Sharp shooters like Lana and Destiny kept watch on the guards, itching for Bienaimé to give the order to shoot. The group was becoming restless, but everyone kept poised, linked by their headsets, anxiously waiting for orders. At last, bright high beams approached from a distance. It was a truck making its way to the facility.

"I'm here," a voice spoke through the headset.

It was Doug; strapped with wires for easy communication with Bienaimé and the others. Doug drove to the main gate and stopped. As he got out of the truck, two guardsmen ran up to him with guns aim ready. With this much hostility, Doug regretted getting out the truck.

"Stay right there!" they ordered.

Doug didn't move a muscle; he knew these guys were taught to shoot first and ask questions later.

"Hey," he said with his hands raised. "My name is Doug Anderson. I'm just here to do a delivery."

One of the guards spoke into his shoulder-mounted radio.

"Watchtower, do we have a delivery by Doug Anderson scheduled for tonight?" he said.

Within seconds, a male voice spoke loud enough for Doug to hear through the guard's radio, "Yes. He's all clear."

"All right, sir, I just need to check what's in the back."

They walked to the back of Doug's truck and opened the door. Before long, they returned and waved up to the tower to open the gates.

"You're all set to go," they informed him as he hopped back in.

He drove to the front of the facility. Ten minutes went by before the entrance door slid open. A slim, average height man in a white lab coat came out. He had flashes of gray in his hair, and bushy eyebrows peeking over the top of his thick glasses. When he spoke, it was with a heavy Russian accent.

"Ahh, Mr. Anderson, I hope you brought my generators this evening," he greeted.

"Yes, Dr. Phils, they're in the back. I just need you to sign these forms, then I can help you get them out," Doug replied, handing him a clipboard and a pen.

"But of course," Dr. Phils said, signing the form and returning it to Doug.

"Okay, guys, we have confirmation," Bienaimé's voice came roaring through the headset. "Adam, scramble their signals. We're going to come in from the back of the building. I need everyone at the back to lock in on a target, and as soon as they move into the shadow, shoot. Do not miss."

Within seconds, muffled shots pierced the air followed by a succession of thuds as bodies dropped to the ground.

"That's about half of them," Zaire radioed in. "Now take out those spotlights before they find the bodies!"

Four men emerged from the woods and ran to the barbwire fence and chopped a huge hole in the chain link with a wire cutter, then slipped inside.

"We have penetration. Snipers provide back up for our guys – if anyone comes near them, take them out," Bienaimé ordered.

The four men took position behind the facility and waited for further instruction.

"I need two snipers to keep an eye on the watch tower at all times. Do not fire until the guards are outside - the windows are bulletproof, but take out those spotlights now," Bienaimé commanded through the radio.

Lana was positioned directly across from the lights. She waited for them to swivel back around, and then squeezed the trigger with perfect rhythm. A guard from inside the tower came running out of the shadows to investigate the sound of glass shattering, but before he reached the spotlight, Lana fired another shot that sent his body tumbling to the ground.

Bienaimé turned to face them, "Good shot, Lana. Cory, Adam, go. Now!"

Cory and Adam sprinted to the fence, slid inside and join the four, hiding behind a brick wall. Activity in the compound was picking up. With communication sabotaged, most of the guards ran toward the towers to investigate the broken lights. Even Dr. Phils made his way over. It was only a matter of time before they discovered the body Lana had shot down, but they already knew something was wrong. The increase of traffic near the main gate left Bienaimé and his men only the slightest risk of exposure. It also became a playground for Bienaimé's sharp shooters.

"Snipers, careful now - Dr. Phils is making his way toward the towers. We don't want him or Doug hurt. Adam, you guys be ready to approach both the Doctor and Doug when the opportunity presents itself." Bienaimé put down his radio and turned to face Lana and Destiny, "Once everyone is distracted, you guys make your way through the fence. I'll have the rest of the sniper team covering you - stay on guard."

*

"That's odd," Dr. Phils grumbled, rushing toward the noise. "What's the commotion over there about? You can never trust these people to do anything right, can't even keep lights working in this shit hole."

"I'm sure it's nothing. The guards should have it under control sir. With this much security, what's the worst that can possibly happen in this place?" Doug asked, trying to maintain his cover.

"You'd be surprised, Mr. Anderson - but I don't mind a little excitement and danger every now and then. My life isn't exactly exciting or vibrant at this point, so I'd like to see what's going on," he replied.

As soon as Dr. Phils was within earshot of the guards, he wasted no time making his presence felt.

"You incompetent fools! What's the meaning of this? What happened here?" he shouted.

His questions went unanswered. The guardsmen were too afraid to speak up and risk upsetting the good doctor further. Looking around, he raised his voice and asked again.

"Well? What is it? Speak up," he barked.

This time, one brave soul walked up and said, "Sir, we're not sure. It could be a burnt-out spotlight, but communication is down, so we're not getting any response from the man inside and the door that leads up to the top of the tower is locked shut."

"Okay, so what's being done about it?"

"We hollered over to the other tower, and someone is making their way down right now with the keys to let us into this one."

Dr. Phils flagged his hand in the air, signaling for the guard to stop speaking. Taking one of the guard's flashlights, he knelt down to examine the shattered pieces of glass. Before he finished his investigation, Bienaimé's snipers started shooting. Their amazing precision – aided by their targets being in the same area, made it more like a game than real life. Destiny and Lana, looking as though they were in a competition, took out the bulk of the guards.

Dr. Phils dove for cover with surprising agility, driven by the whining from bullets flying in the darkness. The guardsmen who were supposed to be protecting him were dropping limply to the ground. The barrage of bullets was deafening; the doctor could hear it, but couldn't see where it was coming from. He lay there in shock, with no option but to observe the madness around him and pray he wouldn't be hit. Digging his face deeper in the dirt, he waited for his demise. Suddenly, he felt a pair of hands pulling him up.

"Get up! We've got to get out of here," Doug yelled over the terror.

Dr. Phils was unsure of what to do, but the fear on Doug's face convinced him he could be trusted. They dashed toward the facility, only to be chased by Cory and his men. Doug didn't hesitate for a second. Turning around, he reached for his gun and shot Cory in the chest several times. As Cory collapsed into the arms of his men, Doug grabbed Dr. Phils by the shoulder and dragged him to the building. Dr. Phils frantically punched a code, and they dove inside as the door slid open.

Inside the facility, most of the scientists had taken refuge behind their desks, and only a few brave ones made their way to the doctor - seeking answers for the chaos.

"This place is being invaded! You could have gotten shot," Doug yelled, full of adrenaline.

Dr. Phils, recovering from his shock, blinked a few times, and muttered softly to himself. Finally, he uttered, "I-I, uh, I need to get something. It's imperative, life or death, actually."

As soon as he spoke those words, Doug knew he had to stay close, so he volunteered to accompany him, and as he was the only one with a gun. The doctor agreed without a second thought.

22

"Fuck! Fuck! Ugh!" Cory screamed, rolling on the ground in pain from the gunshot to his chest. "I'm going to kill that bitch. Oh, I'm going to kill him."

"Cory, are you okay?" Lana asked through the radio with exhausting concern.

"Yeah, I'm good, I-I lost sight of Adam and the others. Doug is in the building with the doctor," Cory said through gritted teeth, trying to mask the excruciating pain.

"Sorry about that, Cory - I got held up with some of the guards," Adam responded, still preoccupied.

"Cory, go on ahead, I'll cover you before I head down. I'll stop the guards, just run inside and go after Dr. Phils," Lana said over the radio. She refocused all of her attention on Cory's position, ignoring the deadly shoot-outs happening with Adam and the others. "Just regain your stamina and go on ahead; I got you."

Vest or no vest, Cory was in agony. It was as if someone had caved his chest in with a metal baseball bat. No matter the pain, he had to move or one of those guards would put him down permanently. *Suck it up,* he thought, staggering to his feet.

"All right Lana, cover me," Cory instructed.

He didn't need to know where Lana was. If anyone had his back, she would. No need to look over his shoulders either - she was always there protecting him from a distance. He ran toward the door, and Lana picked off the guards popping up to attack him. As Cory got closer to his goal, Lana adjusted her scope, and changed to headshots. Even if they couldn't die, she wanted to make sure they didn't stop or hurt Cory.

Cory wasn't fazed when he saw a bullet go through a skull; it was either them or him. When he reached the door, he tried to pry it open, but it wouldn't budge. Desperate to get inside, he fired a barrage from his M16. It proved to be a bad idea - bullets ricocheted off the door, and he scrambled for cover.

"We've got a problem - the door won't open. There's some sort of code panel on the side," Cory radioed in.

"I'll be right there," Adam replied.

Adam came bolting toward Cory. He pulled out a handheld electronic device from his bag.

"Cover me," he said to Cory.

He attached two wires to the control panel. Within seconds, the door slid open with ease. "We're in," Adam radioed in.

"Good job, now go after the doctor. We got these bastards on their heels!" Bienaimé replied over the thunderous volley of gunshots.

23

Quietness descended on the facility. The battle was won, but it was not without its casualties. Ten men suffered massive injuries, dwindling their combat team to fifteen. The resistance was neutralized, and those left surrendered peacefully.

Lana and Destiny entered the research facility, and found Alex interrogating a handful of scientists. They looked scared and confused. Lana found it difficult to believe any of them was diabolical enough to create ATHENS. Whatever their involvement was in The Sabbath, Lana trusted Alex would force the answer out of them.

"We are not here to hurt any of you. We know some of you are here against your will and forced to do terrible and inhumane things…We're here to save you." Alex had a very calming demeanor, and he was utilizing his appearance to this end. His features were so softened; even Lana felt safe listening to him.

"That being said, we need your help - and most of all, your cooperation. We need you to stay put. We have a plan, and it is being executed effectively. All questions you may have will be answered at a later time. Thank you for listening and for your patience as we go through this challenging and difficult experience."

The scientists shuffled as they huddled together. They seemed as if they wanted to protest what was happening, but had no fighting spirit. They just gave up and did as they were told.

Adam and Cory came running in from the corner.

"I need a tablet! Mine got a bullet hole through it. I have to track him because we looked everywhere, and we still can't find him," Adam informed Bienaimé.

Bienaimé left several men to watch over the scientists as he led Zaire, Lana, Destiny, Cory, and Adam to hunt for Dr. Phils.

"Destiny, give your tablet to Adam," Bienaimé instructed. "Lana, you've been analyzing and memorizing the layout of this building for days, see if you can help Adam find Doug."

Adam took the tablet and activated the bracelet. A green beacon flickered on the screen. Lana glanced at the screen and knew where to go. She was surprised how accurate she had imagined the way the place looked. However, finding the doctor proved to be a difficult task. With Adam and Lana guiding, they kept searching.

"Adam and I have already been through here," Cory said.

"Yeah, Lana…are you sure we're going the right way?" Destiny added.

"I'm positive," Lana barked, frustrated and a little annoyed.

"Okay, ladies, let's not let this turn us against each other," Bienaimé interjected, attempting to keep the peace. "Adam, is the communication still down? I don't want them contacting anybody."

"Yes, Professor, the radio signal has been scrambled and anything from an email to a phone call goes to the tablet first for approval—"

"It's here!" Lana interrupted, pointing at the closed door with Dr. Phils' name in big, bold, black font.

"Yes, this is it," Adam agreed.

"All right, guys, not a sound - remember we don't want him to know that he is being tracked. Cory, switch your gun to tranquilizers, and everyone else stay on live ammunition. Cory, you've got the first shot," Bienaimé instructed.

Cory grabbed the doorknob before mouthing, "It's locked." Zaire brushed Cory aside and shot the door open. *So much for keeping quiet.* Cory re-took his position as the head of the group.

Pushing the door open, he poked his head in. The others followed behind, one by one, each covering a section of the enormous, high-ceilinged office with their weapons. It didn't take long to figure out Dr. Phils was not there.

Toggling back and forth from the tracking signal to the blueprint, Lana was mind-boggled as to why Dr. Phils wasn't standing in front of them. Disappointment and exhaustion were taking its toll, and Lana doubted her abilities to find him.

"Shit, this is the last room in this hallway, where else could he be?" Zaire asked.

Cory stepped out to confirm Zaire's statement.

"Yeah, this is the last one," he said, returning to the room.

Everyone was ready to search elsewhere, but Lana refused to give up.

"Wait," she shouted. "Adam, let me see the tablet one more time."

Without a fuss, Adam handed it over. Everyone waited, hoping she figured something out.

"Okay, from where we're standing and the tracking beacon, he should be in front of us, but the blueprint shows that there should be another room over there," Lana said, pointing to the wall.

Bienaimé wasted no time; he hurried to the wall and pressed his ear against it. He knocked on it, while moving side to side. He stopped.

"Someone bring a hammer - I think I've found it," he said.

"Hammer? I got the tool right here - move aside," Zaire roared, raising his ten gauge shotgun.

Bienaimé stepped aside as Zaire fired away. A gaping hole appeared where he had aimed. By the time the dust cleared, Cory had kicked down the wall that remained.

"Look at what we have here," Bienaimé said, looking at the passageway they had just created. "Good job, Lana."

"Thanks Bienaimé," Lana said while giving Destiny a cold glare.

A narrow hallway led to a small, open area. Cory was the first to step inside, and the rest followed. Cory had his gun ready, and as soon as he rounded the corner, Doug materialized out of the gloom and fired. The shot went wild, and Cory returned a few shots of his own. One hit Doug in the chest; the other his forehead. Doug let out a quiet grunt before collapsing. Cory smirked as he stood over Doug. *Too bad these are just tranquilizers*, he thought.

"Ah, Dr. Phils," Zaire said.

In a corner, a man quivered behind a desk in a fetal position, with his head down. Bienaimé approached him, and the rest followed. In a swift motion, Zaire grabbed him, pulling the doctor upright, revealing a metal briefcase handcuffed to his wrist. Dr. Phils stood with his back pinned against the wall, Zaire's hands pressing against his shoulders. His eyes were shut and he refused to open them, as if this would be his end, and he would rather not see it coming.

"Now, what do we have here? Come on, we're not going to hurt you," Zaire smiled.

Dr. Phils shook his head, and said, with his heavy Russian accent, "I haven't seen your faces yet. You guys can still turn around, and I'll forget this ever happened."

Bienaimé laughed, "Come on, doctor; you don't want to see an old friend?"

Dr. Phils open his eyes wide at the sound of Bienaimé's voice.

"You," he shouted. "You did this? How dare you? I'm going to have you killed."

Bienaimé laughed off Dr. Phils' threat, but Zaire took it personally. He swung hard at Dr. Phils' stomach with the back of his gun, sending the doctor back to the ground, gasping for air.

"Now, I told you that we were not going to hurt you, but you couldn't refrain from making those kinds of threats," Zaire scolded, glaring down at Dr. Phils.

"That's enough! Pull him up - we don't have time for this," Bienaimé ordered.

Zaire did as he was told; he pulled Dr. Phils back to his feet, and then sat him down on the desk.

"Ah, that's better. Now, first things first - what's in the briefcase that's so important, that you just had to get it handcuffed to your wrist?" Bienaimé asked.

Dr. Phils glanced down at the briefcase, then grabbed it with both hands and wrapped his arms around it.

"That doesn't concern you," he barked.

Bienaimé thrust out his open hand toward Dr. Phils.

"Give it to me," he demanded.

Hugging his briefcase tighter, the doctor shouted, "No! Like I told you, nothing in here is of value to you."

"Well, if it's all the same to you, I'm still going to have to ask you to hand it over," Bienaimé replied, "or...we can just cut it off, at your wrist."

"You wouldn't dare!" Dr. Phils snarled.

Bienaimé chuckled as he stepped toward the doctor; he leaned forward until his lips were inches from Dr. Phils's ear.

"You're right. I probably wouldn't. But just like you, I have plenty of people who are willing to do my dirty work," he whispered. "Now, let this be the last time you test my patience. I recommend from this point on, you'll do exactly what I say - when I say it."

Bienaimé pulled his face back, seeing that his message had resonated. With his hand trembling, Dr. Phils reached into his pocket and pulled out a set of keys. He took off the handcuff and handed the briefcase over. Bienaimé took the case and set it upright on the desk. A number combination kept it secured.

"What is it?" Bienaimé demanded.

"Two-four-zero-eight," Dr. Phils choked, his voice trembling.

One thing for sure, the doctor was no soldier - not even a shadow remained of the man who had barked orders at his guards. His current situation voided him of the little fighting spirit he'd had.

Entering the code, Bienaimé opened the briefcase. Inside was a large, clear tube filled with crystal blue fluid. Beside it was a syringe filled with a blue substance.

"Well, doesn't this look important!" Bienaimé said sarcastically as the others gathered around to see what he was staring at. "What is it?"

Bienaimé waited for the doctor to respond, but he kept quiet instead. He mustered everything within himself to keep silent.

"Well, what is it?" Bienaimé repeated.

Dr. Phils pursed his lips, struggling not to reply. Bienaimé rolled his eyes.

"We already went over this. Seems like you're choosing the hard way right now," Bienaimé scolded.

Even with the looming threat upon his life, the doctor remained quiet.

"-Guess he wants to do this the hard way, Zaire," Bienaimé said, stepping aside to make room for his colleague.

"Despite popular beliefs, I like the hard way," Zaire seethed as he took his eyes off the briefcase and walked toward Dr. Phils.

With a devilish smile showing his straight, bright-white teeth, Zaire reached into the side pocket of his backpack, pulling out a short black object that fit in the palm of his hand. Looking every bit the predator, he whipped his hand in the air, causing the small object to expand into a long baton.

Once it snapped in place, Zaire whipped the baton in midair several times, each whistle more deafening than the last. Zaire was terrorizing the doctor, who was now a teardrop away from sobbing. He took a big gulp as he braced himself for the first blow — and then came a loud thud. Dr. Phils cried out in excruciating pain before crumbling to the floor. He placed his hands up to surrender, with shimmering tears streaming down his cheeks.

"Please, I beg you. I'll tell you what it is. I am no soldier - I am a scientist. My loyalty is to science, nothing else," Dr. Phils faltered, out of breath.

Zaire scoffed, "It wasn't even worth hitting you a second time, real men don't quiver and cry after being hit once." Before walking away, Zaire spat on the ground near Dr. Phils, showing disdain and utmost disrespect for the coward.

"Zaire may not hit you again, but I have more men who would be more than willing to continue in his place. You've wasted enough of our time. What's in the briefcase? Tell us straight - no more stalling," Bienaimé demanded.

Dr. Phils remained on the ground, but moved from a lying position to sitting on his buttocks. He said, "It's the cure for ATHENS. It's the final product. Perfect, with minimal side effects and completely stable."

No one moved or said anything. For tense moments, the only thing they did was breathe - and only because it was an automatic response.

Lana was too overwhelmed to keep quiet any longer, "Are you serious?" She silently prayed this was the perfect breakthrough, just in time to rescue everyone.

"By the way he tried to protect that briefcase with dear life, I'm going to make an educated guess and say this is the only sample in existence," Cory added.

"Yes, I just stabilized it about a week ago. I still have to wait for more supplies to enable me to make more…there are very powerful people out there, who pay me good money to do what I do - are you sure you want to get involved with them?" Dr. Phils said, still sitting on the ground, looking defeated.

"What are they planning?" Bienaimé asked, ignoring Dr. Phils' warning.

"Like I told you before, I'm just a scientist, they don't tell me about their plans until the last minute. My guess is that they wanted it as a safety net. Look around you; the world is over populated. You need people to die and remain dead. This cure takes away that invulnerability and re-establishes order. One thing I do know is that they don't plan on using the cure anytime soon. Not until they are finished."

"Finished with what?" Zaire asked.

"World domination, of course, order through chaos," Dr. Phils replied matter-of-factly.

"Man, I hate the Government," Lana added.

Dr. Phils laughed at Lana's comment, "I see you have these kids brainwashed too, my old friend. It's not the Government doing all of this - never was. It's the one percent, who are behind all of this."

"For just a scientist, you sure do know a lot. Who's the one percent?" Adam asked.

"Well, I don't pass up the opportunity of new knowledge when it presents itself - and that's the thing, nobody knows who they are. They're the richest of the rich and have been around for centuries, influencing some of the most powerful people. They are the ones who are responsible for the Sabbath, and have encouraged people like you thinking it's the Government so that they can have somebody to blame when things go south...but Bienaimé is right about one thing: in order to stop them, you do have to go through the Government."

"Never mind that right now...how much could you make, and how would you administer the cure to the world population?" Bienaimé asked thoughtfully and inquisitively. His expression showed he was already conjuring a plan to cure the world.

"On a global scale? That would be impossible to determine without going through weeks - if not months - of data. This isn't like ATHENS, where it can go airborne. You see, once the gel is exposed to hydrogen, it turns solid. I was thinking of administration as a form of a pill. The hydrogen does nothing to the formula that I've observed, so I think it's the safest and easiest way of exposure," Dr. Phils explained, still seated on the ground looking up at everyone.

"For god sake, get off the damn floor. Get up and talk to us like a man, even if you have no more dignity left. Pretend that you do!" Zaire interrupted the conversation.

"Pills won't work as effectively as The Sabbath though," Cory said after Dr. Phils was standing on his feet.

"I know," Bienaimé said. "I got an idea, but for now, there's work to be done. Phils, how do we get to the prison undetected?"

Dr. Phils scoffed; astounded that Bienaimé would ask him for anything after torturing him.

"I have no idea," he said, his voice rising.

Zaire pulled out his baton, whipping it in the air.

"Your attitude isn't very becoming. It seems like you still don't want to help us," Zaire said, moving closer to the Doctor.

"No! I really don't know. I don't go to the prison. There's no reason to. If I need someone to test my experiments, the guards bring them to me. I don't leave this building," Dr. Phils exclaimed, afraid that Zaire would strike more rapidly than he could speak.

"Ahh, so they are keeping people captive!" Zaire added.

"Would you have access to the prison?" Adam asked while unlocking his tablet.

"Um, yes. All the scientists do; we just don't take advantage of it. We'd rather have them come to us," Dr. Phils said, looking around at the other people in the room.

"Great, I may have an idea," Adam said, his face lighting up. "Doctor, can you provide us with routes to the prison - as in the most popular route the guards would use to transfer supplies and prisoners back and forth from here to the prison?"

"Perhaps, yes," the doctor replied.

"Okay, this is my plan," Adam continued, "If we disguise ourselves as guardsmen and scientists, we can get inside the prison before they realize anything. With the doctor's help, I'll get Lana to draw up a route that could take us right to the control center, then we'll carry on the same plan we had before."

"That might work," Bienaimé said. "What do you think doctor? What are the possibilities of us being caught before we reach inside?"

"Interestingly enough, the young man is correct. Between this building and the prison, doctors aren't as guarded. We are free to move around without being monitored. Out of good faith, I am willing to accompany you in exchange for my freedom," Dr. Phils bargained.

"Doctor, you don't have a choice - but do good by me, and I'll treat you right. If you try anything funny, then there's a bullet in your head," Bienaimé replied. "Destiny, grab the cure, please. That's yours to protect - and watch him closely... Doctor, if you think you can take her on, think again. If she doesn't shoot you first, she'll definitely cut you, and she aims for major arteries."

As Bienaimé spoke, Destiny closed the briefcase, putting it inside her backpack. She pulled out her knife, waving it at the doctor. The knife was exquisite: the hilt was hand-carved and fit perfectly in Destiny's hand. Watching the light glisten off the curved six-inch metal blade, Dr. Phils's legs went weak with fear as Destiny brandished it in his direction.

"One more, Doctor. How'd you guys do it? How did you guys target the religious people?" Bienaimé inquired. "I've been trying to figure out how you could round them up so quickly."

"Ha! I thought a man such as yourself would have known by now," Dr. Phils gloated. "No matter, I have no objections of telling you my greatest accomplishment." He raised his chin and continued, "In fact, it's the finest achievement ever in science. Nanites were embedded in ATHENS. They were programmed to recognize religious materials- based on keywords and shapes. Once located, DNA retrieved from the objects was catalogued, making the chosen targets easy to harvest. Those that we couldn't capture were reduced to dust by the nanites."

"And the Bible, and other sacred writings, how'd you get rid of that on a global scale?" Lana asked.

Dr. Phils smiled.

"Well, that was a joint effort. The corporation filtered out all apps and religious materials online. Those that remained, the nanites got to them. As far as physical artefacts, the nanites also reduced them to dust."

"You're proud of what you did huh. Well let me wipe that smug off your face," Zaire scolded, raising his hand to strike.

"Enough," Bienaimé said. "Zaire, get everyone ready to leave in five - we'll tell them the plan once we're together."

"Got it," Zaire said, radioing the other members of their team.

Cory bent over Doug and pulled out a set of keys from the unconscious man's pocket, and then tossed it to Bienaimé.

"Okay, let's go," Bienaimé said.

They walked Dr. Phils to the entrance of the building where the other scientists were held hostage. Charles greeted them.

"I see we got what we came for," he said, embracing Bienaimé.

"How are the others?" Bienaimé asked, concerned.

"We lost ten men - one of them took a bullet in the head," Charles answered.

"How bad is it?" Bienaimé asked.

"Brain-dead. Who knows how long it will take for his brain to regenerate - that's if it ever does."

"Shit - and the others?"

"One has broken ribs and can hardly breathe; the others are unconscious probably due to loss of blood."

"How many able-bodied men are left?"

"Fifteen."

Bienaimé paused for a moment, "Okay, leave Alex with three men: two men to watch over the scientists, and one to take care of our wounded. I will send a man to scout ahead to make sure nobody is coming."

Charles wasted no time getting everyone on the same page. Alex rounded up the rest of the guards and grouped them with the scientists. They pushed them into the corner and one by one, shot them with tranquilizers.

"All right, good work! I'll leave the rest to you, Alex. Make sure our soldiers receive medical attention - and keep that briefcase safe! The rest of you, come with me!" Bienaimé ordered.

24

Bienaimé, dressed as a guardsman, jumped into the driver's seat, followed closely by Zaire, also in soldier's attire, and Dr. Phils, still in his lab coat. Charles and Jeff, along with the others, hopped into the back of the truck. Disguised as scientists, each wore lab coat displaying newly appropriated identification badges. They stowed their weapons behind the generator in the truck bed as Bienaimé drove up to the prison gate and stopped.

"You try anything other than what we've discussed, and you'll get a bullet in your head," Zaire said, poking his gun into Dr. Phils' rib cage.

Cory and Lana sat in the back with the others, anxiously waiting what was to come. They knew they had to stay in character or risk sabotaging the entire mission, and their first priority was to get inside. Footsteps of approaching prison guards broke the quiet of the night. The truck dipped from the weight of one of them climbing onto the step bar.

"Gentlemen, it's late, and we're not scheduled for any deliveries. So who are you - and what are you doing here?" the guard asked, scanning the cab with his flashlight.

Zaire gave Dr. Phils a soft nudge with his shoulder, prompting him to answer.

"Oh, sorry, I would have come earlier, but I was caught up with some lab work. The name is Dr. Phils. These two are my servicemen, and I have my scientists in the back of the truck," Dr. Phils said with confidence.

The prison guard flashed the light on Dr. Phils' face before turning it off.

"Dr. Phils, sorry for the guns, but it's protocol. You were not expected."

"It's quite all right. I'm glad to see you guys taking the job serious," Dr. Phils smiled.

"Sorry, but I still have to ask the reason for you being here."

"We have a generator in the back that we need to install in the facility, replacing the old one. State of the art...you know, when technology meets science, it's such a beautiful thing. Anyways, like you said before, it is quite late, and I will appreciate it if we can skip through the formalities and get to work."

"Of course, I'll make sure that you won't run into any more trouble past this point. Let me just have my man check the back."

"If you must," Dr. Phils said, shrugging his shoulders.

The guard signaled for his colleague to inspect the back of the truck. Opening it, he found Cory and the others looking poised and of no threat. He came back and gave his partner a head nod, signaling everything was fine.

"Okay, doctor, you're all set. Where will you be stationed to work?"

"Well, we have to examine the old generator first and go from there. So it might be a two-day job. But I will need access to the building as well as the control center."

"Not a problem, I will notify the guards. All you have to do is let them know who you are, and they will buzz you in. The old generator is just straight ahead near the armory. I'll have someone in the tower flash a light on the building."

The guards opened the gates, and Bienaimé drove on. Soon, they saw a bright light shining on a small building. Once they had reached the building, the light moved away to other areas of the prison.

"Everyone out! Hide your weapons in your lab coat," Zaire radioed.

Zaire and Bienaimé exited the vehicle, making sure Dr. Phils didn't attempt to escape. They led the group inside the unlocked building, and scanned the area for any prison guards and cameras. There was nothing in the building besides an old dusty generator.

"The armory is right beside this dump, eh, well, that makes life a little easier," Destiny said, relieved.

"All right, everyone gather around - we don't have much time," Charles ordered.

Bienaimé gave instructions to the group.

"Okay, there are twelve of us. We're going to be divided into two groups. Charles and Jeff will lead one group, while Zaire and I will lead the other. Cory, Lana, Adam and Destiny, you're with us. The rest of you, with Charles. I need you to stay in this building until I radio in. Then, you guys need to go over to that armory and take it over. Charles and Jeff will have the layout of the prison, so you will be well guided. Remember, stay in character. The longer we go without being noticed, the better. Everyone grab your bags and let's get to work."

This is it. I finally get to see them, Cory thought. He glanced at Lana and the others and found they had the same look of determination. Nothing would get in his way. He would do anything - including sacrificing himself - if it meant his family's safe return.

"Let's go. Cory, stay focused," Bienaimé said. "Zaire, keep an eye on the doctor at all times. We can't afford to lose him now. There are still so many questions that need answering."

Zaire nodded and grabbed Dr. Phils by the arm, placing his lips near the ear of the cowering scientist, "Now you stay very close to me, you hear?" Dr. Phils gave an almost imperceptible nod, and Zaire tightened his grip.

"Yes, yes, I understand," the doctor said with a gasp.

Exiting the building, they headed toward the entrance of the jail. Adam led the way, checking their path on his hand-held tablet. To their surprise, there weren't many guards patrolling the area. They made their way to the entrance without any challenge.

"Okay, what are we facing here?" Cory asked before they entered the building.

"All right," Adam said, in a voice louder than a whisper. "Everyone pay attention. The setup of the prison is relatively simple. As soon as we open that door, it should be the greeting area. And straight ahead is the Control center. Control is located right in the middle, and it divides the prison into four divisions. Past Control," he traced his finger on the screen to highlight two of the blocks, "are the first two divisions."

He tapped the remaining blocks and they brightened, "And here are the other two divisions. So, from left to right, it's four, three, two and one." He paused, giving everyone time to study the layout. After all had nodded, he continued, "Behind the divisions are the prison yards, separated to accommodate the four different divisions."

He looked up from the screen, his voice deepening and said, "It's important to note that division two and three are the largest, which means more guards. One and four are small in comparison."

"What's that narrow corridor between the blocks?" Cory asked.

Adam nodded and said, "That's the pathway between the second and third divisions that leads up to the art centre, and beyond that is the solitary confinement. The infirmary is located right next to it. Got that?"

The group nodded and were at last prepared to walk into the building. Dr. Phils took the lead, with Zaire at his side. They came to an open area with two metal detectors and a prison guard sleeping at his desk. They kept walking, hoping they could get past the man without being noticed. Alas, their footsteps woke the guard from his slumber.

"Hey, hey, hey," he said, startled. His hand moved to his sidearm. "Who are you guys, and what are you doing here?"

"We should be asking you the same thing, officer. Why are you sleeping on the job? But never mind that, I am Professor Wallace, and this is Dr. Phils. We need access to the control center," Bienaimé replied.

"Oh yes, they told me about you guys, go on ahead."

They walked on, being wary of the metal detector. For precaution, Cory already had his hand in his lab coat, clutching his Glock.

As expected, the detector began buzzing.

"We don't have time for this. We have tools in our bags, can we skip the formalities?" Dr. Phils said, hoping to persuade the guard to ignore the detector and let them through.

The guard took a long time looking over them and the black bags they were all carrying. He didn't mind letting them slip through the metal detector, but something made him curious about the bags.

"Sorry, sir, but I need to see what's inside those bags before I let you pass," he said.

"Now you want to take your job seriously?" Dr. Phils scolded, sucking his teeth, his eyes drilling into the man's. Even though his face had reddened, the man didn't back down, and motioned from their bags to his desk.

They placed their bags on the desk and crowded around the officer. Gripping the armrest of his chair, he pushed himself up, and reached to unzip the first bag.

Without pulling his gun from his lab coat, Cory pulled the trigger. All the others heard was a *click* and *thwap*, and the officer slumped back into his seat, his head hitting the desk with a thud.

"Tranquilizer. He'll be out for a few hours," Cory explained.

"Nice," Destiny said, winking at Cory.

Cory turned his head to smile back, but was brushed hard by Lana's shoulder as she pushed past him.

"Let's go," she said, now ahead of the group.

"Hey, Dr. Phils, I was wondering," Cory said as they walked, "why are you being so cooperative?"

"Easy, my loyalty lies with science, and you've got my most precious works in your hands."

"Good to know - maybe I don't have to consider shooting you with this gun every five minutes then," Zaire said, joining the conversation.

Their progress was blocked by a set of locked metal doors. Zaire pressed a black buzzer, activating the intercom.

"Yeah?" a loud voice came roaring through its tinny speaker.

Zaire pulled Dr. Phils around to face him, and raised his gun and brushed the muzzle against the scientist's lips, then pointed it to the button. Dr. Phils cleared his throat and coughed as Zaire roughly pushed him toward the intercom. Regaining his composure, he held the button and with a tone of authority, he said,

"Hi, it's Dr. Phils. We need access to your control center."

"Why didn't Jeffrey buzz you in?"

"Oh, the guard at the front?" Dr. Phils drawled, buying time to gather his thoughts. "I believe he is sleeping, sir."

There was a short pause and then the voice came roaring back.

"That bastard. Okay, I'll buzz you in."

The door unlocked.

Cory was closer to his goal. Every obstacle they had to overcome added more confidence to his character. He felt what he was doing was destined. It became something more than just rescuing his mother and sister. He was fighting a war for the greater good of the world.

They walked to the control center, and were buzzed in. The Center was a pentagon-shaped room, filled with computers and camera monitors. Clear, bulletproof windows surrounded the room- giving the guards a better view of who went in and out. Two guards turned their chairs around, and greeted Cory and the others.

"Welcome! Sorry about Jeffrey - he's always sleeping on the job," one of them said.

"Yeah, he never listens," the other guard agreed. "Dr. Phils, I just want to say it's an honor to meet you. I'm Bruce, and my partner over here is Thomas."

"Nice to meet you both," Dr. Phils replied, shaking their hands. "These are my colleagues who will be helping me out this evening."

"Hi, looks like a slow night tonight," Bienaimé said with a smile.

"It's always like this. Plus, it's eleven o'clock, and everyone is tucked away in their cells, so there isn't much else to do here," Thomas said.

"Well, that explains it. How many people are working here, if you don't mind me asking?" Bienaimé asked.

"We used to have a 250 man staff divided into three shifts, but money is tight everywhere right now. I say we're down to about a hundred guards divided into two shifts," Bruce answered.

"Oh okay, well, I guess we'll get started with what we came to do," Bienaimé said.

"What did you guys come here to do exactly?" Bruce asked. "Maybe we can help."

"We're just checking to see if everything is functional. Just sit back and relax, we'll be out of your hair in no time," Zaire said.

Adam got out his equipment and walked toward the computer system. Thomas turned his chair to supervise Adam, and was shot in the back by Zaire. His body slammed to the floor, knocking his chair on its side. Before Bruce could react, Bienaimé struck him hard with the butt of his gun. Just like his partner, he fell over, unconscious.

"Cory, shoot him. My gun is loaded with live ammo, and it'll be a shame if I have to use it on him," Bienaimé ordered.

Cory shot the guard, then stood back to watch as Adam deciphered the prison computer systems.

"Got it," Adam yelled. "Now, what should I do first?"

"Okay, first things first -can you lock down the prison, and make sure no one goes in or out?" Bienaimé asked.

"Just give me a sec," Adam replied, his fingers flying as he entered a code on his handheld keyboard. "Done!"

"Now on to what we came for…Can you access the database and see where they are holding the captives?"

"I'm doing that as you speak. My Jasmine is being held in division two, cell forty-five. Destiny's Rebecca is in division one, cell sixty-three."

"How about Isabel and my mother?"

"What's their last name?"

"Shembo."

"Okay, I got two hits. Isabel is in solitary confinement and Elizabeth…" Adam raised his head and look at Cory, and continued softly, "Elizabeth is in the infirmary."

Cory's heart skipped a beat, the thought of his mother lying in the infirmary fueled his body with adrenaline. He was on his toes, and his lack of patience was showing.

"Settle down, son, everything will be all right," Bienaimé said, putting his hand on Cory's shoulder, trying to calm him.

Cory wanted to believe that everything would be fine, but he was overcome by what he had felt on the day of her disappearance. He shook his head, trying to get rid of the negativity; he had to remain poised and follow through with the initial plan.

"Charles, Jeff," Bienaimé said through the radio, "you guys can go on ahead and take that armory over. You should have no trouble being buzzed in - tell them you're there to test out the durability of the generator, and you need to see the weapons that they have."

"You think that will work?" Jeff radioed back.

"You're a scientist remember, just sound smart and everything will work out."

"Copy."

Bienaimé turned his attention back to his group.

"All right, here's what we're going to do: Lana, you will go with Cory to get his sister and mother. I'll go with Destiny to get Rebecca and Jasmine. Adam, I need you to stay here - you're the only one who knows how to work this system."

"Oh, okay," Adam said, disappointed he wasn't going to rescue Jasmine.

"Now, let's get rid of the guards first."

"I've got an idea," Cory spoke out, "but we need to scramble their communication first."

Bienaimé urged him to continue, while Adam pulled out another device and jammed the prison's signals.

"Done, it doesn't matter what channel they turn to. It's all static."

"Okay, division three is one of the biggest, right?" Cory asked.

"Yes," Adam answered.

"And can you lock off each division?"

"Yeah."

Cory examined the security monitor and began to strategize.

"Adam, can you use the intercom here and send every guard over to division three?"

Adam grabbed the microphone poking out of the desk and while holding a button, he repeated, "All officers to division three immediately."

With every eye glued to the security monitor, they watched as the guards made their way to the third division of the prison, moving quicker every time Adam prompted on the intercom.

"As soon as most of them are in there, lock the division off," Cory ordered.

Adam sealed off the third division. With their communications down, the prison guard's confusion led to a state of panic, causing them to wake some of the prisoners.

"We took over the armory," a loud voice echoed in everyone's ears.

"Perfect, we're just about to start our operation here. Stand by and wait for our signal," Bienaimé ordered.

"Okay guys, we're on the clock -should be little to no resistance up until this point." Bienaimé pointed at the doctor, "Zaire, watch Dr. Phils for me."

Zaire smiled, and grinned.

"Adam," Bienaimé continued, "we will radio when we need you to open those gates. You guys have these cameras here so we'll need you to be our eyes and ears."

Adam nodded, and said, "Cory, I forwarded the tracking signals over to Lana, just in case you guys get lost."

"Thanks, Adam," Cory replied.

Cory and Lana grabbed their bags and followed Bienaimé and Destiny out. They gave each other a subtle nod, and went their separate ways. Lana pulled out her tablet and glanced at it for a moment, while Cory gave her silence to allow her to focus. She placed the tablet back in her bag, and as she began to jog, she turned to Cory and said, "It's this way!"

They ran until they stood in the middle of a narrow hallway with barely enough room to move around. Nothing surrounded them but barred cell doors, each with another steel door behind it. The lights from the overhead were dimmed; looked more like lit candles than electric light bulbs. They didn't need a sign to know this was solitary confinement. The longer they stood there, the more depressed they felt.

"She should be in there," Lana said, pointing her finger.

"Adam, can you open cell five in solitary confinement?" Cory asked over the radio.

Within seconds, the barred door slid open and the steel door behind it made a clicking sound. Lana stood guard as Cory cautiously pushed the door open. He took a step inside and pitch black darkness consumed him. He couldn't even see his hands in front of his face.

Cory had never been afraid of the dark before, but fear crept into his soul. He shook it off, but the fear was replaced by repulsion from a foul odor. The smell of dead rats and human waste attacked him from all angles. Cory couldn't believe he hadn't noticed it as soon as he walked in. He searched his chest for the wire that allowed him to communicate with the others.

"Yo, Adam, can we get some light in here?"

"Yeah, let me find that for you."

An even dimmer light came on from the overhead. Cory found himself in an eight by ten foot cell with low ceilings. There were no windows or any ventilation, and in the corner was a flooded, metal sink and toilet combo. He spotted a feeble body, balled up on a hard mattress, facing the wall. Cory leaned toward the figure.

"Isabel?" he spoke gently, touching her on the shoulders.

Her body flinched at his slightest touch. Cory pulled her shoulders toward him.

"Bell, it's me, Cory. We've come to take you home."

Looking at Isabel's face, Cory was horror-struck. She looked like death. Her body was bruised all over, with two huge contusions on both sides of her forehead that made it look like she grew out devil's horns. Both eyes were blackened, and one was swollen shut, while the other was reduced to a squint. Her nose was bloody and knocked out of place, and her lips were split and swollen. When she opened her mouth, she revealed bloody stained teeth.

"Cory?" she said, exhausted. "What took you so long?"

Cory let off a light smile as tears rolled down his face. His worst fear was behind him. He was thrilled to finally get his sister back, even in her beaten state.

"Sorry, but it's not easy breaking into prison. I'm so proud of you, Bell… I think it's time you got out of here, come on."

Cory helped Isabel to her feet. She faltered on her first step.

"Will you be able to walk?" Cory asked.

She held tight onto Cory's arms and with her legs shaking, she let out a small grin and said, "Yeah, it's just that I ain't used these in a while."

They walked out the door to Lana, who was already bawling.

"Isabel?" Lana said, lunging her body forward, embracing Isabel while almost knocking her over.

"It's good to see you, too."

"I'm so sorry, Isabel. I should never have left you," Lana said, crying on her shoulders.

"Now, now, my plan worked out fine," Isabel said, patting Lana's back. "A couple of days late, but it worked out fine."

Cory was astonished at his sister's newfound strength. *Wow, to endure what she endured and still be high in spirits. Amazing*, he thought.

"Okay guys, I'm really ready to go home now. I've had it with this place."

"Not yet, Bell," Cory replied. "We have to get mom."

25

They moved closer to the infirmary. As they were about to turn the corner, Adam's voice rang in their ears.

"Stop! There are two guards straight ahead."

Cory stretched out his arm, stopping the others in their tracks.

"What is it?" Isabel whispered.

"There's two men right around the corner," Cory replied, poking his head to see if anyone was coming.

"I thought every guard was in the third division?" Lana whispered.

"I guess not."

"I've got an idea; time to put those lab coats to use," Isabel said.

Cory and Lana turned the corner, with Isabel walking in the middle. She pretended to have her hands tied behind her back while Cory and Lana held her up by the shoulders.

"Hey, can we get some help here?" Cory called out to the two officers guarding the door. Both guards came charging toward them.

"We can take it from here, doctor," one of the guards shouted as he approached.

All they needed was for them to lower their guard. When both officers were in clear sight, Isabel swung her hands from behind her back, revealing two 9-millimeter pistols, and shot the officers to the ground. They didn't want to risk exposure, so Cory and Lana helped drag the bodies behind a wall away from clear sight.

"If it gets hot in there, we'll switch to live ammo, cause these tranquilizers don't put these clowns down fast enough," Cory said, standing over the bodies.

They walked up to a large steel door.

"Adam, can you unlock the door?" Cory said.

"Yeah, she's in room twenty-four - and Cory, stay alert, there are more guards inside," Adam replied.

"So much for little resistance," Lana mocked.

They pushed the door open as they resumed their ploy of Isabel playing possum.

The infirmary looked like heaven compared to solitary confinement. It had high ceilings, and bright lights guided you through the halls. Everything looked clean and in place. As soon as they entered, they found themselves in the waiting area. It was furnished with clear plastic chairs and a round table. There were two guards sitting down, talking. They took one glance at Cory and the others, then returned to their conversation.

There was a reception desk straight ahead with a hospital clerk. She appeared to be even less concerned with their presence than the guards had been. Cory just hoped that they didn't cross paths with an actual doctor. He feared it wouldn't be as easy to masquerade with a real doctor present. They counted up the rooms until they were standing in front of a blue door with a number twenty-four on top. Pushing the door open, they spotted several doctors at a distance, preoccupied with their patients, and a few nurses walking around.

Finding Cory's mother wasn't going to be easy. The room itself was huge, and inside were numerous cubical stations, divided by five-foot walls. Each station contained four hospital beds, separated by five-foot white curtains. Standing up, they had an aerial view of the layout of the floor and the patients in the beds, but Cory's mother wasn't in sight. Taking a deep breath, Cory prepared himself to play a game of hide-and-seek.

"There should be a free bed in the corner," a nurse said as she passed by Cory and the others.

Cory hadn't noticed her coming, but was thankful they fooled her. He waited until she disappeared into a cubicle before giving out his order.

"Okay, we got to split up. Isabel, go with Lana. Radio me when you guys find mom," he instructed.

"All right, we'll take the left side of the room. You take the right," Lana replied.

They went their separate ways, being cautious of the doctors and the nurses. Cory understood the importance of remaining in character, so he walked through the room graciously. The first cubical he looked into had a nurse in it, checking on a patient.

"Don't mind me," he said, stepping into the room.

The nurse turned and gave Cory the same stare you would give a stranger sitting in your living room. However, the puzzled look never deterred Cory's composure. Cracking a light smile, he extended out his hand.

"Dr. Evans, I'm new to the staff."

She paused for a second, letting her brain process this new information. Then she set her clipboard down and shook Cory's hand using both of her hands.

"Hello, doctor, I'm Shantall. Nice to meet you," she said.

"Likewise," Cory said with a smile. "Don't mind me now, I'm just trying to get familiar with the patients."

"Oh, all right, but you look mighty young to be a doctor."

Cory gave out a fake laugh, "Thank you, graduated early…top of my class, too."

"Wow, well, you should get somebody to show you your locker, instead of carrying that big ol' bag around," Shantall said, looking at Cory's black bag.

"Yes, I will after this," Cory said, ending their conversation.

Cory examined the four patients lying unconscious in their beds, and none of them was his mother. Just his luck, he hurried to the other cubicles but still couldn't find his mother in sight. Frustration increased with every passing hospital bed he set his eyes on. He wondered if his mother was even there in the first place. Discouragement crept into his soul, but he refused to give up. As he was about to make his way to another cubicle, Lana radioed in.

"We found her."

Cory's heart jumped with joy as he let out a huge sigh of relief. He twirled his head scanning the entire room, but Lana or Isabel were nowhere in sight.

"Where are you?" he asked.

"We're near the back, I'll stand up."

Within seconds, Lana's head came popping up from the wall, and Cory started speed walking toward them. His anxiety heightened with every step. When Cory walked in, Isabel was on her knees with her back facing him.

"She's right there," Lana whispered while pointing toward Isabel.

He caught a quick glimpse of his mother's smile. Her smile could melt glaciers, the same smile taken away from Cory for too long. He at once fell to his knees, sobbing near his mother's bedside.

"Hi, baby," Elizabeth Shembo said softly, reaching her hand over to Cory.

It filled his heart to see his mother again, but was again saddened by her condition. Elizabeth was lying in bed with countless intravenous needles all over her body. She was bald, and had a scary pale complexion - so much so, that you saw all the blue veins that ran across her body. She had dark circles under her eyes, and the pupils were dull and without color.

Her bones were protruding from underneath her skin, and her fingers had never looked so scrawny and thin before. When she reached out for Cory's hand, her grasp was shaky, and her skin was arctic to the touch. Her speech was slurred and faint and every time she closed her eyes, Cory thought the worst because her breaths were so shallow it made it hard to see the rise and fall of her chest.

Cory was overtaken by emotions. This was the worst he had ever seen his mother, and he blamed himself for not being there for her.

"I should have come for you sooner, mama," he said, still crying and grasping for air.

"Shhh, Shhh, baby, let me take a good look at you."

"You guys found her yet? Everyone's back at the control center, we're ready to release the other captives," Adam radioed in, interrupting their reunion.

One look at his mother and Cory knew she didn't have the energy to walk.

"Adam, can you check the area for any wheelchairs?" Cory asked.

"Not in the room, and you guys don't have the time to look. A guard just spotted the two bodies you guys hid. You guys need to get out of there now!"

"Fuck!" Cory spoke under his breath.

"Watch your mouth," Elizabeth said with a whisper. "Now you guys go on, leave me - you've already given me everything I could ever ask for."

Cory looked around while thinking of a plan to get them safely back to the control center. He unzipped his bag and pulled out an M16 rifle, prompting Lana to do the same. He screwed a silencer onto the barrel of the gun and then handed it to Isabel with his radio.

"Switch to live ammo. Bell, you and Lana have to guide us through this," he ordered. "Mom, I'm not leaving you here, but I'm going to have to ask you to be strong again…Mommy, I need you to be strong."

Cory took off his bulletproof vest and placed it on Elizabeth. Every time her body moved, she gritted her teeth in pain. He then slid his hands underneath Elizabeth and scooped her up. She let out a loud grunt that led to unwanted attention. Cory scanned the room and spotted two doctors making their way toward them.

"Hey, is everything all right?" a doctor shouted.

Cory ignored him and signaled Lana and Isabel to lead they way. Lana nodded as she stepped out the room. Both doctors made their way around the corner and were standing directly across from Lana. Before they could shout for help, Lana pulled her index finger to her lips and warned them to stay quiet.

The doctors dropped their clipboards and raised their hands, but the sound of the clipboards dropping to the floor was like a bomb going off in a quiet room. More heads turned their way as the situation escalated. The sound of footsteps running toward the exit followed. Within seconds, nurses and doctors bolted to the exit, their screams going with them.

"Let them go," Cory said.

Lana set the doctors free and stood watch as they ran toward the door. Doctors and nurses were the only personnel that Lana refused to shoot, and as she walked closer to the exit, she prayed that they wouldn't force her hand. They walked in single file; Lana was in the front, followed by Cory, while Isabel trailed behind, covering their backsides.

"Adam, you've got to lead us," Lana radioed in.

"I gotcha! You guys made quite a noise out there. You've got one guard ushering people out. Two more are trying to contact the control center…and now one of them just ran out the door. Probably trying to make contact manually. I count ten guards who you guys are up against… I'm sending Destiny and the Professor over to you now," Adam said.

"No, go free the others. We got this…what kind of weapons do they have?" Lana asked.

"Standard handgun. Nothing like what you guys have…okay, there's movement now. As soon as you exit that door, there are three guards behind a fixture to the left, and two more on your right. Oh wait - two more are walking toward the door right now."

Lana and the others hid behind a wall and waited for the guards to enter the room. Looking behind them, Lana saw Elizabeth grimacing in pain in Cory's arms. Meanwhile, Isabel shuffled her way to the front near Lana.

"Wait for both to come inside. I'll take out the first one. You'll get the other one," Lana ordered, as Isabel nodded.

"Give up now! We have the building surrounded!" one of the guards said as he entered the room, while his partner followed behind.

Lana took a deep breath and pulled the trigger. As soon as the first body dropped, Isabel shot the other guard down before he could even blink.

"Eight," Lana counted. "Adam, any ideas."

"Have Cory stay back, but take his sister with you and take cover behind the door. Wait there until I give you guys the signals."

They did as they were told, and waited behind the door. Things weren't looking good - Lana knew it would be a miracle if they got out of this one; the only thing that can save them was a genie. Looking at Isabel's face, Lana took in the abuse she must have been through.

"Are you all right?" she mouthed.

Isabel nodded and gave her a shy smile as they continued to wait behind the door. A few minutes went by with the girls not moving a muscle.

Adam's voice radioed in.

"Guys, get ready."

Lana tightened her jaw prepared for action.

Within seconds, all she heard was gunfire.

"Okay, to your left - three guards running toward you, get—"

The girls didn't wait for Adam to finish. Isabel flung the door open while Lana dove out, firing shots at her victims. She didn't bother waiting to see if her bullets hit their marks. Almost immediately, she turned her body around, ready to fire at whoever was behind her. She never expected to find Destiny and Bienaimé smiling back at her as they walked over a guard's body.

Before she could rejoice, Isabel came bolting out, aiming her gun.

"No! They're with us," Lana shouted just as Isabel was about to pull the trigger. Isabel lowered her weapon as Lana let out a big sigh of relief.

"Thanks, Adam."

"No problem, Lana - just don't refuse the help next time, tough guy!"

Adam teased.

When Lana went back into the room with the others, Cory was on the floor, holding onto his ill mother. He was relieved to see Destiny and Bienaimé, and knew he had them to thank for their lives.

"How is she?" Bienaimé asked, concerned.

"I don't know - she has never been this bad," Cory said, holding his mother tight.

Bienaimé took his hand and placed it on top of Elizabeth's shoulders, waking her.

"Hello, my dear," he smiled.

"Bienaimé, it's so good to see you," Elizabeth said with a smile. "Thank you for taking care of my boy."

"You should be proud; you raised a great man. You rest up now; we'll take care of you, then we can finish up our debate."

Elizabeth smiled as she closed her eyes. Bienaimé patted Cory on the shoulders to show his support.

"We have to get her to the control center, out of harm's way - then we can free the others - but we don't have much time. Guards outside are trying to get into the building, and it won't be long before they give up on the radio and send somebody out for help," Bienaimé informed.

"You guys have done enough; go free the others. We still have to take control of this prison, and plus, you guys just cleared the way for us," Cory pointed out.

"All right, you guys hurry now," Bienaimé said as he took Destiny and ran out the door.

"We've got to get going, too," Lana said, urging Cory and Isabel to follow her lead.

"Everything is clear," Adam radioed in as they went through the hallways.

They picked up their speed, not stopping until they reached the control center. Adam and a mysterious woman in an orange jumpsuit greeted them, while Zaire preyed on Dr. Phils in the background.

"Glad you guys made it," Adam said, walking toward them. "How is she?"

Lana stood and watched in awe as Cory and Isabel carefully laid their mother on the ground, using a lab coat as a pillow.

"Lana?" Adam said, hoping to get her attention.

She jolted her head toward Adam and the mysterious woman.

"Not sure, but it's not looking too good."

"Everything will be all right…Oh! This is my girlfriend, Jasmine."

"Nice to meet you," Lana said, offering her hand.

Jasmine smiled and took her hand, shaking it as if she feared breaking it. One glance at her and Lana could tell they had nothing in common. She looked like a blond Barbie doll with the attitude of a diva, and Lana figured that she had Adam wrapped around her fingers.

"Adam, where are the others?" Lana asked.

Adam led Lana to the monitor and pointed at the screen. It was a video of Bienaimé standing on a table speaking to a crowd full of men and women in jumpsuits.

"What happened to the guards?"

"They surrendered once the Professor told them we had control of the building and would free all the prisoners. They're locked up in the cells right now."

"It was that simple, huh?"

"No, not really, it took some convincing, but they had no chance, especially after we opened the cell doors. After a while, they were begging the Professor to lock them away."

"Where's Destiny?"

"She's in the fourth division, talking to the captives right now. I need you and Cory to run down to the other two divisions and update them on what's going on. We've wasted too much time in here already. We need to move fast."

Lana looked back at Cory tending to his mother. Given his mother's condition, it would be unrealistic to expect Cory to leave her side, but it had to be done. She walked up to Cory and with a soft touch on his shoulder, she said, "Cory, we have to go."

Kissing his mother on the forehead, he stood up. "Yeah, I know."

Zaire stopped them right before they left.

"Go take care of your mother - I'll go in your place. Adam, watch over the good doctor."

Cory thanked him and watched as Zaire and Lana disappeared behind the door.

*

"You take the second division; I'll go on ahead and take the first," Zaire ordered as they ran through the halls.

Lana got to the second division and waved good-bye as Zaire ran past her. When she walked in, the lights were dimmed. It was just dark enough to allow a person to sleep comfortably, yet light enough that you could see where you were going. She stood in the center of the floor and took in her surroundings. Barred doors surrounded her. The division had three levels. Each level had thirty-four cells that went around in a circle. There were two metal staircases positioned at the left and right sides of the division. Gazing up at the cells, Lana took the edge of her shirt and twirled it between her fingers.

Her legs buckled.

She had a hard enough time getting Cory to listen to her, and now she had to command the attention of more than a hundred people. She took a deep breath as she radioed Adam.

"A-Adam," she stuttered, "can you patch me through to the intercom and turn the lights on in this place?"

"Yup," Adam replied. "You're good to go; next time you try to radio your voice should echo through the division."

Lana checked her surroundings one last time. The majority of the captives still seemed to be sleeping, but there were a few up and staring at Lana, wondering what was going on. Lana cleared her throat as she prepared herself for her presentation. She shook her head, trying to get rid of the jitters.

"Hello," she said through the radio.

Her voice rang through the division. She heard the rustle of captives getting up and pressing their faces through the barred doors. Whispers started echoing through the room.

"Sorry to wake you, but I came to free you all. There's no time to explain, so I will say this quick. I don't know what they told you, but the Government has captured you all." She stopped twirling her shirt as her confidence grew with each word. "Now, my team and I have taken over this building and the Armory. All that is left are the guards outside. Most of you have loved ones to get to, but if you want your freedom, you're going to have to fight for it. When that cell door opens, I want you to make your way down here and follow me."

While Lana spoke, all the whispers and chattering steadily stopped. The promise of freedom captivated all the prisoners. Lana ordered Adam to open all the prison gates, and when he did, the prisoners made their way to Lana one by one.

"All right, you can start leading all the prisoners near the control center," Adam ordered.

Lana was the first to get to the control center. She made her way inside while the prisoners crowded outside. Soon, Bienaimé and the others came squirming into the room. Lana greeted them and got introduced to yet another mysterious girl in an orange jumpsuit. Her name was Rebecca, Destiny's pretend sister.

"Okay, what do we have?" Bienaimé said as he stepped in.

"Well, we've got a small army versus about fifteen guards outside," Adam replied.

"I like those odds! So what's the plan?"

"Without the weapons in the armory, the guards won't be much of a threat, but there are snipers up in the towers that we can't get to."

"All right, so here's the plan, let the prisoners rush the field outside. They will draw the snipers out, and that's when we shoot. Lana, Destiny, I want both of you to keep an eye on the towers. The first clear shot you get, you take it. Adam, patch me through - let me speak to the prisoners."

Lana and Destiny accompanied Bienaimé out the room to speak to the multitude. It was difficult moving through the crowd, seeing as they packed everyone into the center hall like sardines. The threesome made their way to the front and turned to face the masses. Bienaimé waited until all ears were fixed on him before he spoke. The prisoners were excited and anxious, so it took a few minutes to gather their attention, but Bienaimé never appeared to be rushed for time.

"Everybody, listen up," he started. "Outside these doors are about fifteen men standing in the way of your freedom. The plan is simple: we'll rush them and take control of the prison. Once we have that, we will use their vehicles to get you guys home. Those who know where the armory is located, I suggest you go there first. We have men inside willing to provide you with weapons. I know that many of you are strong in your faith. Well, then consider this as your God sending us here to set you free. You all have five minutes to prepare yourselves; when we unlock that door, it begins."

Bienaimé stopped talking and excused himself back to the control room.

"What happened to the doctors and nurses?" Lana asked Destiny as they walked behind Bienaimé.

"They're safe in a sealed off room until we get this thing over with."

Once they got back into the room, the first thing Lana did was check on Cory. She wasn't sure if he would leave his mother and join the fight outside, but she wouldn't blame him if he stayed indoors. With the small army they had, she was confident they didn't need him out there anyway.

She looked into Cory's eyes, and seeing that there were no words he could have used to express the sorrow he felt, she didn't bother asking him if he was all right. She knelt down beside him and wrapped her arms around his back -that was the only way she could show him that she was there for him. As calm as he looked holding onto his mother, his body felt tense.

"I'm here for you," she whispered into his ear.

26

Cory zoned out, paying little attention to anyone besides his mother. He was so focused on Elizabeth that he almost forgot they were still in prison.

"All right, Adam, get ready to open that door," Bienaimé said from a distance.

Lana leaned toward him, "Cory, stay with her. We don't need you out there."

Just as she stood up, Cory grabbed her hand.

"I'm coming," he declared. "You're not going out there alone. No one close to me is ever getting hurt again. Bell, take care of Mom while I'm gone."

He grabbed his gun before walking out. Bienaimé was in front, preparing the final countdown. Cory, Lana, and Destiny were mixed in with the crowd.

This is it, huh? Cory's mood changed. He felt like a zombie standing in the midst of the living - voided of any care for his own well-being. The weight of the world came crushing down on him. *It would be better if I didn't exist anymore.* He turned his head to the sound and sight of people praying to their gods.

Pointless.

He shook his head in disgust.

Morons.

Mom believed in God all her life, and this is how God rewarded her. If there is a God, he already forgot about us.

Tears rolled down his cheeks, but he wiped them off before anybody noticed.

Turning to Lana, he felt a small flicker of hope return. With everything wrong in the world, Lana embodied everything right, and he felt alive for a moment. He promised himself that he would fight for his mother the same way Lana fought for him.

Get a grip Cory, she ain't dead yet, he thought, chasing away the negativity.

As soon as Adam unlocked the door, everyone rushed outside, yelling and pounding their fists in the air. Bullets greeted the first wave of prisoners, but that didn't stop them from marching on. They kept coming until the prison guards were forced to retreat.

A small group ran toward the armory and returned with Jeff and the others, fully armed. It was chaotic. In the darkness of night, the smell of gunpowder was strong and all Cory could see were flashes coming from the guns.

A beam of light focused on the crowd of prisoners, assisting the sharpshooters in the towers. Using the prisoners as decoys, Cory led Lana and Destiny out, jumping over wounded bodies. He ushered them to cover behind a prison transport vehicle between the two observation towers.

Cory kept watch as Lana and Destiny scanned the towers for the shooters. Meanwhile, the snipers picked apart the prisoners. The tower to the left was so far away the prisoners didn't realize they were being shot at. They scattered defensively, some using others as human shields.

Lana and Destiny hurried to find their targets before they had to retreat to the building. Lana targeted the left tower, while Destiny had already spotted hers in the other. Destiny squeezed the trigger and didn't stop firing until she made sure her victim was neutralized.

Lana was getting frustrated - the left tower had dimmed lighting, making it difficult to get a good visual of the target. *Don't rush it*, she thought, taking a deep breath. She scanned the area once more and found the darker figure of a human body. Making sure her aim was steady; she took a breath, held it, then squeezed the trigger between beats of her heart.

"Fuck!" she cried out.

The bullet missed, passing directly above the figure. Lana watched as her prey repositioned himself in front of the tower door. She vowed to hit him with the next shot.

She took time to calculate adjustment based on the trajectory of the first bullet, made the compensation and sighted in the top of the doorway. She fired, and the bullet hit the figure. Lana fired a few more shots for reassurance.

"Got him," she exalted.

"Okay, now we can go join the others," Cory said.

With the snipers out of the way, it wasn't difficult to regain control. The majority of the guards were already at the mercy of the prisoners, while a few guards fled. They were the lucky ones. The prisoners didn't forgive those who remained. They beat them so bad, that Lana and the others couldn't watch.

Once the battle was won, Bienaimé gathered everyone around him. He suggested each person concentrate on finding transportation. He held up a set of car keys he had taken from a guard, and pressed a button on the key fob. A horn honked, and a light-colored sedan's lights blinked in the parking area. He tossed the key into the crowd. "I don't need to say anything more, people. Good luck, and God speed."

As the former prisoners scattered, Bienaimé led Cory and the others back into the control center. Cory rushed to Elizabeth's side. Her condition worsened. She was in so much pain, she couldn't use sleep to escape it.

"What happened to her?" Cory said.

Isabel looked up at him with puffy eyes and shook her head.

"I don't know," she said, wiping away tears. "She woke up in pain."

Cory surveyed the room. Everyone crowded around his mother with puzzled and concerned looks on their faces. Suddenly, his gaze fixated on Dr. Phils like an eagle spotting its prey. Cory's glare captured everyone's attention, and they turned their heads to see what he was staring at.

If anyone knows what is happening to her, it's him, Cory thought as he took a step toward Dr. Phils. His facial muscles tightened. He played the image of strangling the doctor until he either coughed up answers or coughed up blood. It took one look at Cory, and Dr. Phils knew his intent. The doctor stumbled back to create more space between the possessed man approaching and himself.

"Wait a minute, you can't possibly blame me for this," he cried, his hands extended.

It didn't matter to Cory what the man said. He needed an outlet for his frustration. Zaire stepped between them and tried to calm Cory, but Bienaimé ordered him to step aside and leave him be.

"He deserves answers," Bienaimé said.

Every step Cory took forward, the doctor matched with a step back -

until he was backed into a corner. A quick glance around the room told him no one would rescue him.

"Please, please," he pleaded to Cory.

"Tell him what he needs to know, doctor," Bienaimé advised.

Cory grabbed the doctor by the collar and propped him up against the wall.

"What did you do to my mother?" he shouted.

"L-listen," Dr. Phils stuttered, "I don't know what you're talking about."

Cory released Dr. Phils, planted his right foot back and using his body's momentum, he punched the doctor with a thunderous blow to his chest. The impact of the blow caused the Doctor to collapse onto the floor, his head swaying back and forth gasping for air. Cory stared down at his feeble body, his hands gripping his chest. He waited for the doctor's breathing to return before he continued his interrogation.

Grabbing the doctor by his shirt, Cory dragged his body until he was sitting up against the wall. Pulling up a chair, he sat in front of the doctor. He drew out a small knife with a black handle and toyed with it.

"You're going to tell me what you did to my mother, or I will test that theory of immortality on you."

Dr. Phils sat still, not sure of what to do. His breathing was ragged, and he might have broken a rib. His body flinched at the slightest movement from Cory. He looked at Bienaimé with eyes pleading for help, but Bienaimé turned away from his gaze.

"Don't look at them. They're not going to save you," Cory said with a snarl.

"Please - I'm telling you the truth! I don't know," Dr. Phils sobbed.

"Don't tell me that," Cory screamed, lunging at the doctor.

Just as his blade was about to pierce Dr. Phils's skin, Cory heard his mother's voice calling his name. Although her voice was faint and went unheard by everyone else in the room, to Cory, her voice was clear as day. He took a step back from the doctor, spat at the man's feet, then pivoted on his heel and went to his mother.

"Momma?" he said as he knelt by her side.

"Baby," Elizabeth said, touching Cory's face. "What did I tell you about your anger? You shouldn't let it get the best of you."

"I know, mom, but—"

"It's all right, son...call the doctor over here."

"But—"

Cory stopped speaking. As soon as that word was uttered, he saw his mother mustering all her strength to give him an earful.

"Okay, okay," Cory said.

He stood up, sighed, and then walked back to Dr. Phils. As bizarre as his mother's request was, he didn't dare upset her more.

"Get up, my mom wants to talk to you,"

The doctor let out a huge sigh, glad Cory hadn't returned to finish the job. With pain etched on his face, he struggled to his feet. No one came to his assistance or even looked his way. Straightening his shirt and lab coat, he followed Cory to where his mother lay. He much rather preferred talking to someone who couldn't do him any harm.

He knelt down next to Cory's mother. She beckoned him closer, so he placed his face near her mouth as she whispered into his ear. Cory drew out his gun and stood guard. One wrong move meant a bullet in the back of Dr. Phils' head. The doctor pulled his head back and crawled a few feet away from Elizabeth. He stood up slowly, running his hand through his hair, and looking down at the floor.

After a moment, he asked Cory, "What was her condition before ATHENS?"

"She had cancer; it was bad, but never like this…" Cory replied.

"I see. Well, my department never ran tests on her. We only chose those who were fit. Your mother would never have made it through the screening process. Was she going through chemotherapy?"

"Yes, she was."

"All right. The thing with ATHENS is that it only sustains life - it doesn't improve it. If your mother was still going through treatments, she should never have stopped."

The doctor saw Cory's jaw tighten, and took a step back. His voice had a whining, defensive tone as he continued, "This prison doesn't have the facility to treat cancer patients. Her staying here with no treatment has led to her current condition."

"Okay," Cory said, closing the gap between them. "How about your cure?"

"I'm afraid it won't work." Beads of moisture appeared on the doctor's forehead. "You see, the only thing that's keeping your mother alive right now is ATHENS. If she takes the cure, then without a doubt, she will die."

"Give it to me," Elizabeth commanded with all the strength she had.

"No, Momma!" Cory barked back before returning his attention to the doctor. "There's got to be another way!"

"Cory," Elizabeth said, calling her son.

"Yes, Momma," he said, returning to her side. He blew out a few quick breaths that did nothing to relieve the pain in his chest. He forced himself to look into her eyes, not wanting to hear what he feared she might say.

"It's okay, son. My time has come. I don't have to be strong any more; I don't have to suffer any more—"

"No, Mommy, don't talk like that!" Isabel cried.

"Shhh-shhh…let me have a good look at you both…my you've grown, Cory. You take good care of your sister now; don't let anyone touch her face like that again." Elizabeth turned her head to look at Isabel. "Bell, my beautiful girl. Be strong for him, he'll need you. There's nothing more I can give to the both of you. It's time for me to be with the Lord." With that, she closed her eyes and relaxed, her face looking peaceful for the first time during the day's long ordeal.

"Where's the cure?" Isabel asked, turning to the Doctor.

"It's safe with the other group," Bienaimé answered. "Let's get everyone into the truck and get out of here. Cory, I'll pull the truck up, and then you can come out with your mother."

As the others exited the room, only Cory and Isabel remained with their mother. They held each other close and took comfort in the silence. When the time came, Cory scooped up Elizabeth in his arms and carried her outside, and two men helped him place Elizabeth into the truck.

They made her as comfortable as possible on the flat metal surface, and Cory cradled her in his arms as they drove back to the camping site to regroup with the others.

Chants of victory from a group of huddled people greeted them upon their arrival, but Cory felt more defeated than ever before. Elizabeth had drifted to sleep during the ride, and Cory gently slid from under her, while Isabel moved into place and held her close. Hopping out of the truck, Cory joined Lana, and they followed Bienaimé to greet Alex.

"Ahh, welcome back, glad everything went well," Alex said, shaking Bienaimé's hand.

"Yes, just as we planned," Bienaimé replied.

"Where are the prisoners?"

"They all scattered home, but we have a way to find them when the time comes."

"Perfect - and the doctor?"

"— Still in the truck. Do you have the briefcase?"

"Yes, it's right here," Alex said, lifting his hand. "There's one more thing…"

Bienaimé studied Alex's face for a moment, sensing he had discovered something disturbing while at the research facility. He waved at Jeff, Zaire, and Charles to join them. They spoke in low voices, so the others in the camp wouldn't hear.

"It's even worse than we imagined, Bienaimé," Alex said.

"What? Explain what you mean," Zaire demanded.

"I hacked into Dr. Phils' secured files, and the biometric chips aren't meant for the general population," Alex continued. "The targeted population are the folks inside the cities. And the chips are lethal. If not for our healing abilities, these chips can kill by short-circuiting the human brain."

"And they just developed a cure to neutralize that ability," Bienaimé added.

"My God," Lana said, covering her mouth to stifle the scream she felt might escape. She looked up at Cory, "What about Grandma?"

She had made up her mind not to leave Cory, but now she wanted to get her grandmother out of the city. Cory wrapped his arms around her, lending her his strength.

Bienaimé gave them a moment, then said, his eyes full of compassion, "Darlin', we can't deal with troubles that aren't yet here. Let's take care of one thing at a time." He motioned to Alex to continue.

"The research facility was using the prisoners as test subjects. Keeping the sick in dire conditions to test out the full capabilities of ATHENS. The rest of the prisoners underwent a series of experiments." Alex paused and glanced over his shoulders. "We don't know their plans for us 'regular folks', but we can't trust the prisoners. Some of them already have the chip implanted in their skull."

They stood silently for a moment, considering the implications, until Bienaimé rallied them once more. "We've got a lot of work to do, but first things first." He took the briefcase from Alex, and said, Thanks. I'll explain later." Turning, he handed it to Cory. "Go, get this to your mother."

Cory took the case. Taking Bienaimé aside, he said, "Not right here, not like this. I want to take her home. Can I use your car?"

"Sure, son. Now go to her," Bienaimé said, giving Cory his car keys.

Cory took the keys and passed them to Lana. Going back to the truck to get his mother, he saw Dr. Phils being watched by one of Zaire's man. There was something he needed to ask.

Walking up to the doctor, Cory pulled him on the shoulder, forcing him to turn around.

"Back there, what did my mom whisper in your ear?" he questioned.

"Nothing...she thanked me for keeping her alive," Dr. Phils answered.

Releasing the doctor, Cory started walking off when Dr. Phils stopped him.

"I see you have the cure...so you will use it on her after all."

Cory glanced down at the briefcase, a look of great sorrow on his face - and then there it was - Dr. Phils' sudden change of heart.

"I-I'm sorry," he said to Cory, clearing his throat, "I can tell she was a good woman."

Any man could have looked in his face and known he was sincere. Cory nodded before disappearing into the truck.

"We're taking her home," he said to Isabel as he climbed in.

Lana drove up and honked. While Isabel held the briefcase, Cory carried his mother down the loading ramp and into the backseat of Bienaimé's Mercedes. They laid her down, letting her head rest on Isabel's lap. Once they were all settled, Lana drove out.

The ride back home was smooth. Lana never sped. She wanted to give Cory and his sister as much time possible with their mother. Once they were home, Cory lifted his mother out of the car while Isabel rushed to open the front door of the house. Lana held the briefcase with one hand, using the other to draw out her weapon and keep watch. One look at his mother's face and Cory knew he'd made the right decision in bringing her back home. Elizabeth rejoiced when she was finally put to rest on her own bed.

Lana stood in the corner of the room while Cory and Isabel tended to Elizabeth. She didn't want to intrude, so she kept to herself. She pushed aside the urge to leave them alone in the room; she couldn't leave Cory - not right now.

"Oh, it's just as I remember. It's so good to be home," Elizabeth said with a smile. "Lana, come here, dear."

"Yes, ma'am," she said, walking over.

"You have been a blessing ever since you came into my son's life. You're heaven sent, and I hope he can see that. Thank you, baby - for being a part of my family."

Elizabeth's spirit was high. Although she felt discomfort, the pain was now tolerable as she spoke her last good-byes. She made sure nothing was left unsaid as she expressed the love she had for all of them. By the time she had finished, not a single dry eye remained in the room.

Settling back into her own bed, propped on her pillows, Elizabeth said softly, "Okay, Cory, I'm ready."

The briefcase felt heavy and cold as he set it on top of the bed, and popped it open. With trembling hands and tear-blurred vision, he froze - staring at the syringe now lying in his hand. He had no way of knowing how much time his mother would have after he injected it. All he knew was that she would be gone forever.

Cory began shaking all over as images of his dying mother plagued his mind. Seeing his distress, his mother reached out for his hand and grabbed it, her grasp firm and full of conviction.

"It's all right, son, put everything in God's hands."

"God?" Cory cried out. "How can you still utter his name, Momma? After all you've been through? Where was he to protect you? You worked your body to— "

"Cory," Isabel yelled, trying to calm him as Lana took a step closer.

"Shhh-shhh," Elizabeth hissed at Isabel. "Let him go."

"Momma, every day you woke up and did everything according to his word, and what did you get out of it, huh? Cancer? And now you're forced to die. I can't accept that. If there is a God, why do bad things keep happening to us? There is nothing but bad things in this world!"

Elizabeth's heart broke as she felt her son's pain. Her eyes were like puddles; her lips trembled as she gathered her thoughts and searched for the right words to leave with her son.

"Baby, I'm sorry I wasn't rich and had to work like I did. I'm sorry my body was weak, and I got sick. I'm sorry your father left. Baby..." Cory, close to collapsing, knelt down and laid his head on the edge of the bed, and she stroked his hair. "Cory, don't blame God when the person you really want to blame is me."

Cory lifted his head and opened his mouth to object, but she shushed him and continued, "I'm leaving you today, don't be like the others and not take ownership for what you do. God doesn't let bad things happen in this world; we do. Give him the glory."

Elizabeth looked at Isabel, then back to her son. "Cory, when I had cancer, I was dying. Chemo wasn't working. I prayed every night for God not to take me away from you unless I knew you were going to be all right. Every night, son, I prayed for him to give me the strength to see another day."

Cory rocked back onto his heels, tears streaming down his cheeks as Isabel and Lana stood helplessly behind him.

"Now look, the effects of my cancer have been postponed, and I finally get to see that you can take care of yourself. More importantly, you're doing something special…it was all worth it, son. Now please give me the gift of death. Don't deny me God's final blessing."

Cory cried and cried until he had no tears left. He looked deeply into his mother's eyes, and whispered an apology to her. Summoning every ounce of courage he had within him, he took the cap off the syringe.

"Momma, I love you."

"I know, son. I know…"

Taking a deep breath, he slowly injected the contents into his mother's forearm as Lana moved in closer.

"Come, Isabel, pray for me," Elizabeth said, holding onto her children's hands. "Close your eyes, Cory - you too, Lana."

Isabel said a quick prayer, and then, one by one, they all opened their eyes - except for Elizabeth. Cory shook his mother's lifeless body, desperate to keep her with them longer. He wouldn't have stopped shaking her if Lana hadn't restrained him.

"She's gone, Cory," she said, holding him tight.

Breaking free from her grasp, Cory bolted to the corner and collapsed to his knees; his head sunk onto his chest as he pounded his fist on the floor. His tears found their way back to him, and flowed without ceasing. His heart shattered, and he mourned and felt himself close to dying from grief.

Then, in an instant, clarity flooded his mind. He understood his mother's death was a precedent, not just for him, but also to the rest of the world. She wasn't coming back to life like the others. No - she was gone for good, and no matter how loud Cory begged for her; nothing could bring her back.

Sensing a change in him, Isabel hugged him from behind, and Lana embraced them both. They stayed there, side-by-side, grief stricken, consoling each other.

"You don't' have to be strong right now," Isabel pleaded with Cory, crying. "This time I will be there for you."

*

A few hours after the death of his mother, Cory acted like she wasn't gone. Lana thought he was taking his mother's death well - even being strong, maybe - but she was wrong. On the outside, Cory seemed okay, but deep down inside, his body burned with rage - angry with anyone who had taken a part in his mother's passing, including himself.

That night, he did not sleep. He was numb. It was his body's way of dealing with the disbelief he was experiencing - disbelief that his mother was laying lifeless in the next room. In the morning, they buried Elizabeth in the backyard. Dressed in black, they each stood still, saying their last good-byes.

"Get some sleep, Cory," Isabel said, walking back into the house.

Cory nodded, but remained where he stood, holding onto Lana. An hour went by, and not a word was spoken. Finally, Cory looked down at Lana and said, "Can I get a second alone?"

"Sure," she replied, squeezing his hand, then returned to the house.

Cory remained in silence for a moment before looking up above.

"God," he shouted. "I don't know if you're there, but I need you."

He stood there, letting his words resonate as if he was talking to someone on the physical plane. He blew a kiss to his mother, then turned around and headed inside. As he entered the home where his mother had raised Isabel and him, he knew he would soon have to leave it behind.

Cory took one last look at the small patch of disturbed earth in the garden, his lips turning up in a grim smile, and swore on her grave all who were responsible for The Sabbath would get what was coming to them - starting with Dr. Phils. The death of his mother brought out a consolation prize: vengeance.

THE END

ABOUT THE AUTHOR

Arthur Nsenga is a college student completing his Masters in Political Science at Carleton University, Ottawa. He writes stories to escape the torments of his college professors. When he is not writing or cramming for a test, he is adding new content to his website @ www.arthurnsenga.com.

ABOUT THE AUTHOR

Shaunakay Francis is a recent graduate from Carleton University. Although she has a degree in psychology, she has had a passion for writing for a long time, having published several poems. Now, having completed her undergraduate studies, she plans to immerse herself more in her writing.